Cold River

Imagine just three months of your life, not safe at home but lost in the forest in the dead of winter; three months of struggling against unceasing odds, with only the memory of a parent's last words to give you the help and strength to fight for survival.

Elizabeth Allison was thirteen and her step-brother Tim a year younger when their father decided to show them how to live in the very depths of the wooded mountains of the Adirondacks. What began as an exciting canoeing trip suddenly turned to disaster with their father's fatal accident. Before he died, he had begun to tell them how to live in the wild: only to eat red meat with fat, to strangle turkeys with their bare hands, how to use spruce boughs for beds. By the time the November snow sets in, Lizzie and Tim are ready to fight for their survival, able under severe stress to use their hands and their heads to their fullest capacity.

But their father has not prepared them for the one really big unknown – another human being.

Other titles in Fontana Lions

A Question of Courage *Marjorie Darke*
Ride the Iron Horse *Marjorie Darke*
Nobody's Family is Going to Change *Louise Fitzhugh*
The Owl Service *Alan Garner*
M. C. Higgins, The Great *Virginia Hamilton*
A Sound of Chariots *Mollie Hunter*
When Hitler Stole Pink Rabbit *Judith Kerr*
The Other Way Round *Judith Kerr*
The Power of Stars *Louise Lawrence*
The Year of the Black Pony *Walt Morey*
Z for Zachariah *Robert O'Brien*
Path of Hunters *Robert Newton Peck*
The Borrowed House *Hilda van Stockum*
The Pigman *Paul Zindel*

and many more

WILLIAM JUDSON

Cold River

FONTANA LIONS

First published in Great Britain 1974 by
Talmy Franklin Ltd
First published in Fontana Lions 1979
by William Collins Sons & Co Ltd
14 St James's Place, London SW1

Printed in Great Britain
by William Collins Sons & Co Ltd, Glasgow

This story is dedicated to
my own sweet Lizzy

ONE

The River

Now that I am older than my father, I think I understand why he always treated me the way he did. He wanted a son, but I was born instead and the doctors told him that Mama should not have any more children, so he was stuck with a daughter. Since I was all he had to work with, he did the best he could. I don't mean to say that he sat down and figured out that was what he *should* do — my father was never one for sitting around thinking when he could be moving around doing. Everybody knows that. Mike Allison was head and shoulders the best guide and outdoorsman in the Adirondacks, and what's more, he would flatten the head of anyone who disputed it.

I looked down at the Adirondack Mountains this morning. A plane was taking me from Albany to Buffalo. The snow covered almost everything below, but the big pines made black patches against the lightness of the land, and here and there I could see open water where a big lake had started to break up without waiting for the spring thaw.

All country looks the same from a great altitude. I had one of the best views in the airplane. The stewardesses always seem to think it is my first time in an airplane and outdo themselves making me comfortable. I am not as old as they think; my face is, I confess, ten years older than the rest of me, and that makes me look around seventy to those young, fresh, fragrant girls who run up and down the aisles serving coffee and milk and stronger potions to those who want them.

I have never been a drinker myself, although for some years there after the Second War, I had word that Timothy had turned to the bottle. After what we had been through together, this saddened me. Later, I learned that the stories were only half true, and I felt a lot better. Though Timothy is only my stepbrother, we have loved and trusted each other ever since that terrible winter in 1921. We've taken different paths in life, but it has always been a comfort to me to know that somewhere there has been a person who would drop everything and fly to me if I ever became ill or found myself in danger. Of course, I would – and have – done the same. In the matter of Tim's drunkenness, I soon learned that these were merely stories being circulated by his jealous wife in hopes of securing a large divorce settlement, that while Tim had perhaps been out on the town with the boys on one or two occasions, he was anything but a habitual drunkard. I put that lady straight, I can tell you. After I was done, Mrs High and Mighty was lucky to get fifteen dollars a week temporary support. We Allisons have never been much for higher education and fancy clothes, but when trouble comes, we stick together.

I do not know how many millions of acres there are now in the Adirondack Mountain Preserve. Despite the constant efforts of the land developers to chop it up for their profitable schemes, the country there has been declared 'forever green.' Even with the politicians whittling away at the charter, I think that it will remain so. Our world has shrunk so small that even the greediest of us are forced to see that it is high time we stopped destroying that which cannot be replaced in our lifetimes. In Albany, where I live and work, I am known as the Dragon Lady of the conservationists, a nickname that doesn't bother me a bit. I have bearded Mr Governor in his den, as well as those mealy-mouthed little senators who buzz around, hoping to get kick-backs from the developers.

The *New York Times* once put my photograph across three columns of their second section when I smuggled a nesting blue heron into the governor's office and set her up at housekeeping. She nested there for three weeks, until the eggs hatched. There were many who laughed and poked fun at me. The governor was fit to be tied, but I made my point. A swamp-drainage programme near Watertown, which would have disturbed thousands of nesting birds, was not approved. I still have the newspaper clipping, which says, in part:

Elizabeth Allison, sixty-year-old nature enthusiast, confronted New York's governor in his office yesterday and defied him to remove her and a matronly blue heron from his chambers. Miss Allison, a longtime supporter of conservation measures, was once (1921) the subject of a statewide rescue operation when she and her younger brother, Timothy, were lost in the northern Adirondack Mountains during the dead of winter.

But this is apart from my story. What I want to tell you is about Timothy and me, about the mountains, and especially about that winter of 1921 when, as the *New York Times* says, we were lost in the dead of winter.

I saw that frozen country again beneath the wings of my jet airliner this morning. It took only a few minutes to fly over it and leave it behind.

But in 1921 it took Timmy and me nearly three months to cover the same distance on what I now call our 'interrupted journey.'

As I said, Tim was my stepbrother. My real mother died when I was three, and a few years later, my father married Pauline Hood, a widow, with one son, Timothy, who was a year younger than me.

Father had met her down in Speculator on a trip to buy winter supplies, and they came to live with us on Indian Lake. Now that there was a boy in the house, I could devote myself to my dolls and needlework and piano lessons. I didn't, of course. Most people are quick to learn two things about me. The first is that I remember every word I hear. The most casual remark is burned into my memory for all time. This mysterious gift should have been enough to carry me to untold glories were it not for my other outstanding trait which can only be described as pure bone laziness. I never run when I can walk, walk when I can stand, stand when I can sit, or sit when I can lie down.

But the harm had already been done. Those years my father had alone with me wrought permanent harm. While I may have complained a lot, there was never a fishing trip or an overnight camp-out that did not finally draw me, like a fluttering moth to its compelling flame. By the age of eight, when seven-year-old Tim came to live with us, I had already become what I am today: a hopeless lover of the great outdoors.

It soon grew into a competition between my stepbrother and me. He could run faster, but I knew the shortcuts. He was stronger, but I knew how to use a lever. He could swim faster, but I swam farther.

We fought, and Tim always won. He was stronger. I *could* have won, but that would have meant using a trick or a hold or a fall that might have broken bones, and I decided no fight was worth it.

My stepmother, Miss Pauline (which is what I called her), was a strong, drab woman whose only interests lay in the kitchen, the garden, and the bank. She was very money-conscious, which did my father untold good, since he was the most improvident man in the Adirondacks. In those days he could get nine dollars for a first-rate beaver pelt, and trapping the stupid creatures was easier than falling off a log, but somehow my father never got around to putting in his trap line until the neighbours had already staked out the best ponds. Indian Pete, our next-door neighbour who lived two miles up the road, was the best trapper in the country. He could throw a deadfall together from an old log and some saplings and a bit of twine in two minutes flat, and next day, when he ran his trap line, there would almost always be a fox or a rabbit trapped under it. Once, when I went with him early on a Christmas morning, we found a skunk. That was the first time I ever saw Pete angry. He mumbled a string of remarks in Mohawk and used a precious cartridge to dispatch the skunk.

'Why are you so mad, Pete?'

'Skunk, him ruin fox runway. All poisoned. No more fox come here.'

'But isn't a skunk hide worth money?'

'Two dollar. Bad cleaning. Stink up knife, stretching board.'

With distaste he picked the skunk up with a split tree branch and dropped it on to a page of newspaper he took from his pack.

'Why don't you just throw it away, then?'

He shook his head. Pete's hair was long and shiny black and hung down around his shoulders. 'No, Missy. Killum, skinum. No throwum away.'

This was my first lesson in conservation. It has always stuck with me. *Take what you need, use it all, and leave something for the next person.*

Until Tim came, Pete was my only friend. I went to school down in the village, but we were too far out of town for the other children to visit us often. Sometimes I rode Charlie, our plough horse, when he wasn't needed in the field, but usually I walked. Today, going from our old house to the centre of Indian Lake takes less than five minutes by car. In 1921, walking down the lonely dirt road took Tim and me more than an hour, carrying our schoolbooks tied in an old belt and our lunches packed in brown paper bags. Bags were scarce, too, so we never threw them away, but put them in our classroom desks to take home again. Eventually, they became so stained with grease that we were ashamed and would hide them from our schoolmates who had fancy lunch boxes made of tin. When the bags were so far gone that nothing could persuade us to take them to school one more time, Miss Pauline would put them aside for my father. Then he would catch a mess of wall-eyed pike, skin them, wrap them in the greasy bags, and put them in the oven to cook. An hour later the bags were all dry and crumbly, and the fish were moist and flaky under the fork. They melted in your mouth.

9

I have never really understood Daylight Saving Time. I don't remember whether we even had it then. All I do remember is that as winter came on, the days became too short for us to get out of school and reach home before dark, even when we ran part of the way. There was always snow by then, and our boots squeaked on it. We didn't need much light to see our way; the moon and stars were enough. If the sky was overcast, we followed the ruts and sang songs to cheer ourselves up. We talked, and I told Tim stories that I had read and could recite word for word. I would tell him an episode each evening. Sometimes when the story was coming to an exciting part, we would see the kerosene lamp shining through the windows far ahead, and slowed down so I could finish that part before we got home. Or, if I was feeling mischievous, I might take Tim to the part of the story where the adventurers hear something in the underbrush, then I would take off and run for home as fast as I could, with him chasing me. We had a rule — if he caught me before I got inside the front gate, I had to sneak down the hall to his room that night, after my father and Miss Pauline had gone to bed, and finish the story.

It was nice to have someone to talk to, and although (as I said) we fought a lot, Tim and I were true friends. He stood up for me at school, where some of the other kids got unruly when I always won the spelling bee and the other contests that called for memory. Oddly enough, my grades were not very good. Although I could remember every word I heard, I did not always understand and so often fell into error by repeating, by rote, what I had learned without understanding how step A related to step B and how both affected step C. The teacher, who had to control the first six classes all in the same room, was alternately delighted and distraught by me. He dreamed of having a nation-wide spelling winner but despaired when, after having recited a difficult series of verb declensions, I was unable to use any of them in a rational sentence.

'Elizabeth Allison!' he would sputter, 'you don't know your lesson.'

'You told me to memorize it,' I would answer sweetly. 'I know every word.'

'But you don't *understand* what you're saying,' he would choke. Still he was on shaky ground, and he knew it. Few of his other pupils really understood what they had absorbed so painfully by rote, either.

The only time I did not like going to school was when Tim was sick. This happened often, for, despite his active outdoor life, he was not strong. He always had a cold or a fever or some kind of rash. Then I would hurry home, trying to outrace darkness and always losing. The curse of a vivid imagination is when night comes and you are alone on a country road and the tree branches are creaking in the shadows. The flap of an owl's wings will stop your heart, and the shriek of a dying rabbit is enough to put rockets on your heels. When I staggered, gasping, into the kitchen, my father laughed at me if he was there.

'Is the Devil after you?'

'I heard something in the woods.'

'There is always something to hear in the woods, Lizzy.' My father always called me Lizzy, and so did Tim. Everyone else called me Elizabeth.

'Anyway, it was cold.'

He would laugh. 'Lizzy, Lizzy, haven't you heard anything I taught you? Nothing in the woods will hurt you unless you hurt it first.'

'That may be,' I said. 'But perhaps I might hurt it without meaning to. I don't believe in taking risks.'

This would always send him up the chimney. I was just a little girl, yet I always talked like an old lady. That was because once something was in my head, it stayed there, and I had been reading all kinds of fancy books where people talked that way.

Also, we listened to the radio. It was a funny-looking contraption, not like the radios you see today, or even like the ones we had before television. It had an earphone that you held up to your ear. There was a little control that moved a piece of metal they called a 'cat's-whisker' over a piece of quartz. When you found the station, the quartz would sometimes hold steady for as long as five or ten minutes. Then you had to hunt for it again. I had a favourite station. At six in the evening a man would give the news in a deep mellow voice. Since the station was more than a hundred miles away, I regarded the radio as nothing less than miraculous and used words I had never heard before, words like 'situation' and 'prognosis' and 'kilocycle.' My father did not approve of the radio and never listened to it. Miss Pauline had brought it with her, saying that one day it would be the entertainment of the world.

'No more going down to Indian Lake just to see a travelling Punch and Judy show,' she would tell us. 'It will come right into the home, free of charge, for all to enjoy.' My father laughed at her, and at the time, I thought he was right. Except for the mellow-voiced man at six in the evening, there was precious little that the radio had to offer me.

In 1920 my father bought a used Tin Lizzie. I think he paid $350 for it. Noisy and bone-rattling though it was, that Ford Model T changed our lives. Now we could go all the way to Speculator for shopping without spending two days on the road with the old wagon and Charlie. Once there, we even had time to rest a few minutes in the nickelodeon, watching the latest Little Mary Sun Play. I think that's what they called movies in those days. When I see our rugged outdoorsmen today with their $6,000, four-wheel-drive Jeeps and Land-Rovers, tons of metal and complicated wiring, I have to smile as I remember our Model T. It stood seven feet tall, knock-kneed and bony. Only its mother could have loved it. But it would go anywhere and run on anything. If it was sluggish, you simply tossed some camphor balls in the gas tank. Or if you couldn't get gasoline, it would run on kerosene and chopped-up candle wax. Neither hole nor hill stopped it. Almost *all* driving then was 'off road,' and our old banger opened up new lakes and streams to my father's fishing rod and trap lines. The Model T would follow old cattle trails and footpaths. It could wend its way through a pine forest almost as easily as a white-tailed deer, yet it was so light that if it dug its way into a bog, four men could pick it up and carry it to firmer ground. The tyres weren't much bigger than bike tyres. By the time my father bought the car, there were some four million Model Ts in the country, and more and more of them were finding their way into our mountain wilderness. Everybody had a joke about them. One man was supposed to have asked that his flivver be buried with him because, 'I ain't never been in a hole yet where my Model T couldn't get me out.' Spud Wilkens, who ran the garage in Indian Lake, said one traveller came in and ordered a pint of gas. 'Don't you think it ought to have more than that?' Spud asked. The traveller replied: 'No, I'm weaning it.' More than once, I saw Fords go by with college boys in them, up our way camping, with stickers pasted on the side reading, 'Danger! 50,000 Jolts!'

By 1921 my father had become very concerned about the growing number of tourists in the woods. 'They're going to ruin the fishing,' he predicted. 'And they'll drive the animals so far upland that we'll never shoot another deer.'

Of course, he never considered giving up his own Model T. It had opened up too many new trails for us. He just didn't want anybody else poaching on the wild land he considered to be his own. Now, Miss Pauline, she never went out into the woods with us. She didn't really approve of Tim turning into an outdoor boy. But she never said anything to my father; she knew better. Besides, what was Tim supposed to do if he grew up without knowing how to act in the woods? Work in an office in the city? A man had to work outside; that's the way things were.

She took a stronger turn with me, though, but I dug in my heels and held back. I didn't mind learning the stuff girls were supposed to know, because deep down I knew that some day I would have to do those things for my husband and family. It was never ever suggested that I might not end up with a husband. So I had to prepare myself. But those home things came easy to me and still left plenty of time to tag along after Tim and my father, which I did.

My father was a good teacher. He seemed terribly old and wise to me then, but now that I am older than he was when he died, I know that he was really a young, vigorous man in his mid-thirties – trim, powerful, firm in his opinions, loyal to his friends and a relentless, unforgiving enemy – traits and attributes that were not uncommon in young men of that day. He believed in punishment and reward. If I broke a fishing-rod or lost a hook by accident, it was nothing to fear. But if I did so through carelessness, it meant a switching, and not any I'm-sorry-I - have - to - punish - you - and - this - hurts - me - more - than-it-does-you nonsense either. He laid on the fresh-cut branch hot and heavy.

I would not be alive now if it weren't for the things my father taught us, Tim and me. We would have died in a matter of days, alone in the forest, that winter, if he hadn't prepared us. Today, when I read about someone lost in the woods, I shiver and pray for him, for not one in a thousand is trained for the woods. The woods are full of hikers and campers and fishermen who lose themselves with a regularity that keeps the newspapers full of headlines. I wonder why they are permitted to endanger themselves when no state lets a fool with a car on to the road unless he can pass a test proving that he knows how to drive. So many city people feel that just because the woods belong to all of us they must rush out straightaway to grab their share before somebody else gets it, and in so doing, they come to grief. As you know, and as the governor in Albany will attest, no one has been more vigorous in protecting those wild lands that should be held in trust for future generations than Elizabeth Allison, but I must shout 'halt' when I see the foolishness of some of the people who would visit the wilderness unprepared. It is as if they somehow feel that those of us who live in the rough are stupid and unskilled and that our knowledge is so easily acquired that it can be got out of a book skimmed in one afternoon in a comfortable lodge before setting out on foot or by canoe or horse. Not so. I stand here to bear witness. My father was one of the finest guides the north mountains ever produced and still the wilderness killed him. What hope will your soft city dweller have with his guide book?

Well, that's enough about me. I have been speaking with you at such length so that you would know who I am, and how I feel about certain important matters. If you don't know Lizzy Allison by now, then you have been glancing away from this to watch television and losing track of what I have been saying. It's not important whether you like me or not. What *is* important is that this story show you how things used to be in the woods and that you understand me.

In 1921 there was no such thing as long-range weather forecasting. We were lucky if the newspaper was right about today's rain. The *Farmer's Almanac* told us it would be a dry summer or a wet spring or a cold winter. Somehow it was usually right, although Miss Pauline poohpoohed it, claiming that it was an entertainment provided for the edification of manufacturers wishing to sell soap and patent medicines. Anyway, the *Almanac* promised us that the winter of 1921 was going to be a bad one, with early snow, heavy freezes, and a severe winterkill.

Winters must be warmer in the city – and no wonder, with all those furnaces and automobiles spewing smoke and steam high in the air. Why, one February day when my father drove us all the way to Albany, you could see the smoke rising above the city nearly ten miles away, and when we got inside the city limits, the snow was melted off the streets and the gutters ran wet. Back in Indian Lake, we were still driving on two feet of ice.

The city newspapers (which is, after all, the only place big papers are published) weren't worried about the coming winter, but my father was. He had consulted the *Almanac* – but more important than that, he had been watching the forest and had decided that we were in for a bad one.

'The geese are flying a month too soon,' he said, pointing up at the honking 'V' of southbound birds. 'The deer are already out of their summer coats, and the rabbits are starting to turn white. We're in for an early winter, and a cold one.'

Miss Pauline was knitting. 'We'd better lay in plenty of firewood,' she observed.

My father pulled at his chin the way he always did when he was thinking. 'Don't worry about that,' he said absently. 'I made a deal with the Birns brothers. They're bringing over thirty cord, and they'll stack it too. I promised them enough hides to bring sixty dollars down to Speculator.'

'If we get plenty of snow, the trapping will be good,' Tim said. Tim was twelve, and I had just turned thirteen. I remember the date, too. It was October 3, 1921.

'Not true,' said father. 'The signs say we'll get a hard freeze before snow flies. Once the frost gets in the ground, snow'll come too late to blanket and keep the cold out. All the roots, the tubers, the buried food will be bound in. The young trees will die. The apples and berries will be frozen solid. No, Tim, I think we're going to see a bad winterkill.'

'What's winterkill?' I asked. I knew, but I could see that Tim didn't, and he wouldn't ask. He was stubborn that way.

My father smiled at me. I always loved his smile. We didn't see it often, but when we did, it lit up the whole cabin. He knew what I was up to but didn't give me away.

'Well, Lizzy,' he said slowly, 'that's when winter comes on so sudden and so fierce that the animals aren't ready for it or can't protect and feed themselves, and most of them die. Your deer herds will make yards to spend the winter in back in the woods, and as the snow deepens, they'll climb up on it and eat away at the trees, but no matter how much snow we get it won't be enough and one by one they will starve and die.'

'How awful,' Miss Pauline said.

My father shrugged. 'It's just nature,' he told her. 'We
don't have any say-so in it. But I'll tell you this – I
intend to lay in four or five extra deer carcasses once we
get a freeze. We can hang them in the barn. The deer are
going to die anyway, so we might as well eat them.
Besides, we may be snowed in here ourselves for a couple
of months.'

Miss Pauline's eyes widened. Winters had been hard,
but there had never been any talk of getting snowed in
before. 'Maybe we ought to move down and stay with
my sister,' she suggested.

My father made an impatient movement with his hand.
'It ain't no hardship, being snowed in, not if you're ready
for it. I been snowed in three times before.'

'But the children,' said Miss Pauline. 'Their school.'

'We've got plenty of books,' he said. 'You can read
their lessons, if worst comes to be. I'll guarantee you
this : they'll learn more good from a winter like that than
they will from a hundred books.'

'What happens to the rest of the animals?' Tim asked.
He rubbed his hand across his nose, which was always
too small to suit him and which had landed him in about
two fights a week with boys who called him 'Pug'.

My father looked at him just like he was another man.
'It's bad,' he said. 'The bears go to their caves too soon,
so they can't make it all the way through the winter,
and they have to come out and go hunting for something
to eat. That's the only time I'd ever be afraid of a bear,
when he has to come out of hibernation early. The same
thing happens to the birds. The turkeys will starve. We'll
take some of them too. You know I don't hold with poaching, Tim, but this here's different. Since they're going
to die anyway, it's only common sense to use them to
help us instead of letting them go to waste.'

'What about the ducks and geese?' I asked.

'All depends. They've already started south. But seems
like there's always a bunch that don't leave soon enough.

17

They'll find our lakes frozen and no forage. I've seen the lakes freeze up fast enough to catch them by the legs overnight. Then the foxes come out and feed.'

Miss Pauline said: 'How can you be sure from just a few flock of early geese?'

'Can't really say. Man gets a feeling just like the other animals. Can't explain it, can't talk it away. It just happens. How do the geese know when to fly? They just do. I've seen them go over when it was so hot it'd melt butter in the springhouse. Next week, we'd get a hard freeze. They *know* – and so do I.'

'Animals have instinct,' she said. 'I don't hold with that in man. Man is a superior being. He is ruled by reason and logic.'

'Be that as it may,' my father said, 'but we're going to have us an early winter, and it's going to be a long, hard one. There's going to be a winterkill such as we ain't seen in twenty years.'

'All right,' Miss Pauline agreed. 'We'll have plenty of wood and food. I have faith in you, Michael.'

He looked down at his shoes. 'What I've been meaning to say, Pauline, is that this may be the last year we'll have a chance to see deer herds the way they are now. If we get a bad winterkill, it'll bring the herds down to nothing, and by the time they build up again – say five, six years – we'll have so many tourists you won't be able to find a beaver dam without ten people standing on it clicking their Kodaks.'

'What are you getting at, Michael?'

My father looked at me and then at Tim. 'I'm thinking about the kids,' he said. 'Times are changing. Things will never be the same again. I saw it coming, but I hoped that Lizzy would be grown and married before we ever had to admit it.'

'Admit what?' Miss Pauline asked.

'That we're outdated. We're country people in a city world. Another twenty years and this country is going to be concrete highways from one end to the other. Henry

Ford will go down in history as the man who ruined the US of America.'

'I notice you still drive your Ford,' she said, smiling.

My father grinned back. 'If you can't lick 'em, join 'em. But our time is coming, Pauline. Before then, I want our kids to have something to remember.'

She put her knitting aside. 'The canoe trip,' she said. 'You've still got that on your mind.'

This was the first I'd heard of any canoe trip. I looked at Tim. He shook his head. He didn't know either.

'My father said: 'If they're going to see the way this country is and have something to remember, the time is now. The winterkill this year will hit the wildlife so bad, it won't come back, not soon enough to do Tim and Lizzy any good.'

'They've seen deer,' Miss Pauline said. 'They've seen every animal there is. You've seen to that.'

'Only what hangs around near the farms. That's nothing. Pauline, you don't know what I'm talking about. You've never been out there. You've never seen a flock of ducks so thick they made the sky dark. You've never seen a herd of deer covering a valley like a brown carpet. You've never dropped a hook in fishing water so good that the trout'd bite on a piece of white shirt.'

'Is all that so important?' she asked evenly.

'It is to me. And I think it's important to my kids.'

She opened her mouth, and for an instant I knew what she wanted to say – that Tim wasn't his real son. My father knew too, and he stared her down. She closed her mouth without saying it.

Instead she picked up her knitting again and said softly. 'When do you want to go?'

'Next week,' he said. 'If I have your say-so, that is. You know I wouldn't go against your wishes, Pauline.'

She waited a long time before answering. When she did, there was something in her voice that I didn't recognize at the time. Today I would know it instantly as anguish. 'Michael, what choice do I have? I know how important this is to you. How could I deny you when this goes so close to the bone? But I'm afraid. I'm always afraid when you go into the woods with a client, so you must know how much more afraid I'll be when it is with my . . . my children. So much can happen.'

'Nothing will happen, Pauline,' he said, hugging her, happy that he'd gotten his way so easily.

'How long will you be gone?'

'Week, say ten days.'

'They'll miss school.'

'Let them.'

'You'll take care?'

'You know I will.'

'And you won't take chances?'

'Pauline,' he said carefully, 'I never take chances. Ask anybody. I never had a client so much as sprain his ankle.'

'I know,' she said. She reached out and touched his cheek. 'I realize how important this is to you, Michael. I only wish it were that important to me.'

'I don't blame you,' he said. 'We've all got different things we have to do.'

He turned to Tim. 'What shape is the canoe in?'

'Good,' said Tim.

'Need any pitch?' The canoe was made of canvas, and the seams were sealed with pine pitch.

'Maybe a spot here and there.'

'Better take care of it. I don't want any leaks.'

'Father,' I said, 'am I going?'

He turned to me. 'Do you want to go, Lizzy?'

'Yes.'

'It's going to be a hard trip. We'll have only what we can take in the canoe. The bugs will be biting.'

'I don't care,' I said. 'If Tim's going, I want to too.'

'Do you want to go, Tim?' he asked.

Tim didn't have to answer. He was jumping up and down.

'All right,' said my father, 'but it ain't all going to be fun. There's lots of work to be done. We've got gear to stow, supplies to plan, and we don't have much time.

You're both of age to pull your own weight. I don't want any kid stuff. No fights, no arguing.'

Tim said, 'Thank you, Dad. I'll do my part.'

'I will too,' I said.

My father smiled at us. 'I know you will,' he said. 'Well, what's the hold up? When do we eat?'

My stepmother got up and started putting supper on the table. Maybe it was where I was sitting, maybe it was only the reflection from the fire, but I was sure that she had tears in her eyes.

These days, camping is so simple. But think for a moment how it was fifty years ago. We had no plastic, no way to waterproof food or anything else. There were no down-filled sleeping-bags – at least not for poor people like us. We made do with blankets held together with safety pins. There were no pump-up gas lanterns for light. We used stubby candles with an oiled-paper shade. We didn't have fancy Coleman stoves either. We cooked over a wood fire. Our utensils were one heavy Dutch oven and a skillet blackened by many seasons of camping. We had a flint and steel, but my father had taken three hundred kitchen matches and poured melted candles over them so they were encased in a waterproof block of wax that ought to see us through a dozen trips. Freeze-dried meals? The nearest thing to that were the dried pinto beans that would be our staple food, along with the fish we would catch and the game we would shoot. Our fishing gear was basic. No spin casting rods or fibreglass poles. We had a couple of hundred feet of heavy twine and some hooks. We would cut our poles as we went. Probably the only item of gear we had that was better than the equipment most people have today were our knives. Each of us had a four-inch hunting-knife, hand-forged by Harry Perkins over in Deer Creek and sharpened to a fine edge on my father's whetstone. Our boots were raw leather, uninsulated. Our clothing was rough, heavy wool – uglier than today's Dacron but much warmer, especially when wet. We wore itchy long underwear, the kind that legend says pioneer children were sewn into from October until April. It kept us cool on warm days and warm on cold ones. Our hats, by today's standards, were ugly, flop-brimmed messes, but they kept off the sun, and the rain didn't run down our necks. Tim had his single-shot .22 Winchester rifle and fifty rounds. He had paid for every single round himself with money earned helping the farmers bring in their hay. My father had a five-shot .44 Colt, with a long barrel, and a 30-30 rifle wrapped up in an oil-soaked rag. I wasn't allowed a gun, although I could recite ballistic tables of all the major calibres from reading them in my father's gun books. We had no tent, just a heavy canvas fly that we could hang from four trees to keep off the rain. Our jackets were heavy, brown wool with bright patches. When wet with rain, one could weigh at least twenty pounds. But they kept out the cold and the wind.

Oh we were a ragamuffin bunch, no sight for your posh camping magazines. But we were equipped to survive. Everything we carried had a use and had proven itself time and again. The only addition was our Tin Lizzie, which had never been as far into the woods as my father intended to go.

He hung a map up in the kitchen and went over it with us and Miss Pauline.

'We'll take the Model T in on that old logging trail to Beaver Creek,' he said. 'We'll drift down Beaver Creek, two, three days, and that ought to bring us to Big Wolf Lake. We should see big deer herds all along the way. We'll hole up on Stag Island for a couple of days – fish, enjoy ourselves, then pack out to Tupper Lake. I'll leave the canoe on Big Wolf, keep it there for fishing next spring.'

'How will you get the Ford out?'

'When we get back, I'll borrow Hod Taylor's truck, and Pete and me'll drive in and pick her up.'

Miss Pauline ran out of questions. My father had thought out every part of the trip with great care.

As we prepared, I noticed, now that I was looking for them, signs of the impending winter. The big bullfrogs,

22

which had serenaded us all summer with their bassy *ker-chunk*, had almost vanished, gone into muddy hibernation. The autumn foliage was at its brightest. The birch leaves were bright yellow, and the oaks were flaming pillars of red. The wild grape vines behind the barn were heavy with blue clusters dusted with grey powder. Tim and I ate them until we got a stomach ache. Traffic to the outhouse was heavy for a few days. After that first purple-fingered, juice-stained-mouth orgy, we moderated our attacks on the vines and picked several buckets for Miss Pauline to make into jelly. Our pear trees were bowed under fruit, and wild birds surrounded the windfalls in black swarms. We gathered more than enough for canning, until Miss Pauline cried, 'No more!' and still there were pears rotting underfoot.

I marvelled at the wisdom of nature – and of my father. Some days the temperature rose to ninety-five, and in the hot evenings the katydids filled the air with song. The lightning bugs were out, too. Tim and I caught them and filled a Mason jar, and they gave off enough light to read by. Winter seemed so far away that it was inconceivable, yet my father was hard at work preparing for it. So were the animals in the forest.

The day for our departure came closer. The preparations were nearly complete. I still found it hard to believe that we were really going. This new adventure was more than either Tim or I had hoped for. Usually when the weather was good enough for such trips, my father had a client for fishing or hunting or simply exploring. But this time, he turned them down in order to have the time for the canoe trip.

'I'm not going to discuss it,' he told Miss Pauline. 'You know how set on this trip those kids are. I couldn't take it away from them.'

'But Mr Heath is one of your best clients,' she said. 'He pays good money, and there's always a bonus. Besides, the sugarbowl's nearly empty. We could use the extra money this winter, Michael.'

'We'll make do for the winter,' he said. 'I told you, I'm

not going to argue. If we run short later on, I'll go down to Speculator and hire out for wages. But I won't go back on my word about the trip.'

She knew when to stop pushing, and did.

The days were long now. In the daylight still left after school, Tim and I explored the woods near the cabin. We were excited about the canoe trip, but that was a week away, for ever in our children's sense of time.

This was the autumn that we first really investigated the fuzzy bear caterpillars. It seemed that as the winter approached, each caterpillar caught a bad case of itchy feet. And since each had a hundred feet, the itching must have been tremendous. The fuzzy bears were all over, engaged in some private migration to a destination known only to them. Nothing would lead them astray. Tim and I picked up dozens, whirled them in circles, carried them down the road hundreds of yards from their original location – and when we put each fuzzy bear back on the ground, it would twist its woolly head in a circle, unlimber its soft body, and point itself towards where it had been going in the first place. We put one in a cardboard box and shook it up until it couldn't have known which way was up, and soon as it was secure on the ground, it re-oriented itself and set off towards its goal again.

'I think he's got a compass built into his head,' Tim said.

'That's silly, he's only a caterpillar.'

'All right, Miss Smarty. How do *you* explain how he knows where he's going?'

'He doesn't. He's just crossing the road.'

'But you can't get him mixed up. He always crosses it in the same direction.'

'Maybe he memorized that big oak tree over there.'

'Then how come he still crosses the same direction when we take him down by the pond – There aren't any trees at all across the road there.'

'I don't know,' I said.

'Well, I do,' said Tim. 'He's got a compass in his head.'

Like I said, there was no arguing with Tim. When he

thought he was right, he would never admit that he was wrong, even when the evidence went straight against him.

That night my father sat us down after supper and talked for a while about going out in the woods and getting lost.

'Tim can't get lost. He's got a compass in his head, just like that fuzzy ol' bear caterpillar.'

My father frowned, and I scooched down in my chair. He was going to talk serious.

'All right, Tim,' he said. 'Let's say you wandered away from camp and got turned around and the next thing you knew, you were lost. What would you do?'

'I wouldn't get lost,' said Tim. 'I don't care what Miss Smarty Pants says, I *do* have a compass, and I know how to use it.' He took it out of his pocket, the genuine fluid-damped direction finder he had earned by selling subscriptions to *Munsey's Magazine*.

My father smiled. 'You could have forgotten it,' he said. 'Or maybe you fell down and broke it. Tim, too much pride is a dangerous thing. Everybody who goes in the woods often enough is bound to get lost sooner or later. The difference is, the real woodsman gets out without much trouble, while the tenderfoot only gets in more trouble and somebody has to go fetch him. Now answer me.'

Tim thought for a moment. 'Well, if I knew I wasn't more than a mile or so from camp, and you or Pete was there, I'd just sit down and light two smokes fires.'

'How would you get the smoke?'

'I guess I'd use curled up birch bark and dry wood to get a good hot fire going, then I'd throw rotten wood and grass over it.'

My father nodded. 'That's very good. But what if you didn't have matches?'

'I'd use my flint and steel.'

'You left that in camp.'

'Then I'd make a fire bow and get some embers glowing by whirling a stick in a piece of pine punk.'

25

'Yes,' my father agreed, 'it's not easy but I've seen you do it. But let's say it's nearly dark and you don't have time to build a fire.'

'Then I'd use the sun, if it was up, to get my direction. If it was night, I'd watch the stars.'

'It's overcast.'

Tim was running out of answers. He squinted at the middle distance as if reading the answer on the kitchen wall. 'I suppose I could get north by the moss on the trees,' he said.

'No, boy,' said my father. 'That only holds true for a big tree standing by itself out in a field. In the forest, the moss can be on any side of the tree. The light's all diffused, and there's no steady wind, so the moss grows any which way.'

Tim thought again. 'Well,' he said, 'if you or Pete knew I was missing, the best thing would be for me to just stay where I was. If I got to wandering around in the woods, we could miss each other. But if I stayed put, you'd come on me a whole lot easier.'

'Fine.' My father turned to me. 'Lizzy, now *you're* lost, and there's nobody in camp. Nobody's going to come looking for you, and you've got to get out by yourself. How do you start?'

'Find water,' I said.

'Easier said than done,' my father answered.

'Walk downhill until I cut across a fresh game trail and follow it to a stream.'

'How do you know you aren't going the wrong way?' Tim asked.

'If the trail's getting stronger, I'm headed towards water. Once I find the stream, I follow it until it cuts a trail, which it always will sooner or later.'

'All right,' my father agreed. 'Now, how will you know whether you're headed in or out on the trail?'

'I'd watch where other trails joined it. If they branch off in front of me like a 'Y', I'll be going into the woods. But if they come *in* in front of me, like an upsidedown 'Y', then I'm headed out.'

My father looked at me quietly. 'That's very good, Lizzy. Where did you learn that?'

'I heard it once.'

'Do you remember everything you hear?' my father had never paid much attention to my schoolwork.

Miss Pauline broke in. 'The girl remembers every word she hears. Trouble is, she doesn't always understand what she remembers.'

My father shook his head. 'That's a new one.' He lit his pipe and exhaled smoke. 'Well, I'm right proud of both of you. I think you'll do all right.'

Miss Pauline put away her knitting. 'Time for bed now,' she said.

We said good night and went off to bed.

But I couldn't go to sleep for a long time. I lay there in the dark, wondering what it would be like to be lost in the woods.

Looking back, knowing now what was to happen, it would be easy to fall into the trap of thinking that my father had some supernatural instinct about the future and had therefore set out to prepare us for the ordeal of our interrupted journey. But I don't think that was so. He was a professional guide, accustomed to taking nothing for granted. He knew from having lived with us that Tim and I were at home in the woods, but that was not enough, for my father was a careful man. He set himself to reinforcing our knowledge.

Our canoe was a fifteen-footer, hand-made from canvas and mountain ash by our neighbour, Indian Pete, who had traded it to my father some years back for two boxes of shotgun shells and an axe. It was wider in the beam than the usual Indian canoe, nearly fifty inches. Consequently it was stable in waters that would roll a more narrow craft. Pete had made the canoe without the usual centre thwart, so it wasn't possible to carry it with two paddles lashed to form a yoke. But in the Adirondacks a wooden yoke has long been used to carry the heavy guide boats. It can be adapted to canoes, which is what my father did. He cursed it in a gentle way, too, because when the canoe was over his head on a long portage, it tended to sway like a seesaw, which it wouldn't have done with lashed paddles.

The canoe weighed a little over seventy pounds. When one morning the week before we were to leave, my father told me he was going to show me how to portage it, I couldn't believe him at first. I have always been strong and wiry, but it didn't seem possible that I could hoist that long canoe over my head and walk through the woods.

'You take it slow and easy, Lizzy,' said my father. 'I don't see any chance of you having to carry the canoe on this trip, but just in case, I'd like you to know what to do.'

I bent down and took hold of the bow. My father stopped me. 'One step at a time, or you could hurt yourself. Let's pretend that Tim is with you, but he's broken his arm and can't carry anything. Still, he can help you turn it over.' He nodded to Tim. Together, we rolled the canoe over.

'Now, Tim,' my father said, 'get your good arm and shoulder under the bow and lift it up until it's propped on your head.'

Pretending that his right arm was broken, Tim grunted and strained and got the canoe up at a forty-five-degree angle without much trouble and kept it propped there.

'All right, Lizzy,' said my father, 'step underneath and get the yoke over your shoulders. Bend your knees, not your back. That's it. Now stand up.'

I did, and to my amazement, the canoe bow swung up and balanced on my shoulders. I took a careful step and, although it swayed, the canoe stayed where it was supposed to. It didn't even feel too heavy.

'Carry it down to the barn and back.'

I heard Miss Pauline draw her breath in quickly. My father said: 'It's not too far for her, Pauline. Now you keep your thoughts to yourself or you'll make her lose confidence.' I started down the path, moving slowly. The weight wasn't what bothered me. I was afraid I would let the canoe tip and fall off. But it didn't, although it swayed alarmingly when I made the turn at the barn. I got back to the road without difficulty. Tim stepped under the bow and together we lowered it to the ground.

'There,' said my father, 'I'd reckon you carried it some sixty yards. Most portages aren't any longer than that. If they are, you just prop the bow up against a tree catch every now and then and get some rest, then get on about your trip.'

Lifting the canoe by myself wasn't any harder. My father showed me how to pick up the bow, get it shoulder high, and inch my way back until suddenly the canoe fell forward, balancing on the yoke. I trotted down to the barn and back again, this time with more confidence. Then Father made Tim go through everything, and I laughed when he let the canoe fall as he made the turn near the barn. But he got it up on his shoulders by himself and completed the 'portage.'

'How long until supper?' my father asked.

'An hour,' said Miss Pauline.

'All right, we'll be back by then.' He led us into the woods, stopping only to pick up his camp axe. Miss Pauline didn't ask where we were going.

As we walked down the path between the pines, my father told us: 'We're going out to have a good time, not be miserable. And since we're going to spend around eight hours every night in bed, let's make sure our beds are comfortable. Tim, what do you suggest?'

Tim looked at the axe. 'A browse bed, I guess,' he said.

'How do you make one?'

'Fell some spruce boughs, spread them out for a mattress.'

'That's the idea, but that's not the way,' said my father. 'If you want a browse bed to be really comfortable, you ought to thatch it. But first, let's find a good camp site. Never mind about water, we'll forget that. But other than water, find me a site fit to use.'

We looked around. I found a sloping hill and pointed it out. 'This looks nice,' I said.

My father laughed. 'You'd roll out of bed and down that hill the first five minutes,' he said. 'Look, here's what we want. A nice dry, level piece of ground without too many rocks. You two, gather up what there are. Save them for the camp fire.'

As we pried stones out of the ground, my father found a deadfall and cut four poles. Two were around seven feet long; the other two were half that length. When we had the ground ready, he laid the poles down in the shape of a bed, seven feet long and four feet wide, and drove pegs at the corners to hold them in place.

'Now,' he said, 'let's find us a nice evergreen. Balsam's best.'

'There's one over near the slope,' said Tim.

We went over, and my father cut another pole. 'You hold this, Tim,' he said. Then he began cutting small boughs and draping them over the end of the pole. The needles interlocked and held the big pile and boughs in place. When they got heavy, Tim carried them over to the 'bed' and came back for more.

When he thought he had enough, my father began spreading them between the four poles, the heavy butt ends pointed down at the foot of the bed. Each layer covered the bare ends even deeper. When the 'mattress' was finished, it was more than a foot thick. My father gave us smaller boughs, and we poked them in wherever we could find a hole.

Father threw down his jacket to keep the needles from poking us, and we took turns lying down.

'It's softer than my corn husk mattress at home,' said Tim. Tim had the only corn husk mattress in the cabin. Mine was feathers, and so was the one in my father's bedroom. Every time Tim turned over in the night, you could hear the husks whispering together.

My father laughed. 'A bed like this is good for two, maybe three, nights,' he said. 'Then you've got to add fresh boughs to fluff it up again.'

'Are we going to sleep on browse beds?' I asked.

'We sure are,' said my father.

'They look like they might itch,' I said.

He laughed. 'We'll have our sleeping blankets to take care of that, Lizzy. You'd better worry about the black flies, instead.'

'There won't be any black flies,' Tim said positively.

My father looked at him. 'How do you know?'

'It'll be too cold,' said Tim. 'I bet it'll even be too cold for deer flies.'

I shuddered. 'I don't like deer flies.' One had bitten me on the arm during the summer. It was just like having a chunk taken out with a pair of red hot pliers.

'Neither do the deer,' my father said. 'You ever watch them flicking their ears and their tails? Those darned deer flies chew on them something awful.'

'What good are flies, Dad?' asked Tim.

'They have their place,' said my father. 'Without the flies and other insects, the birds wouldn't have anything to eat. It seems that for every critter God put on the earth, he put another one to torment it. The deer flies bite the deer; birds eat the flies; and the fox and wildcats eat the birds.'

'And men eat foxes and wildcats,' I said.

My father gave me a strange look. 'Yes, Lizzy, I suppose you're right,' he said. 'Man is the only critter without a natural enemy. His only enemy is other men.' He picked up his axe just as the dinner bell rang down at the cabin. 'Come on, dinner's hot, and your mother'll skin us if we keep her waiting.'

Time dragged. But suddenly it speeded up, and almost before I knew it, it was October 14th, and we were leaving early the next morning. The Model T was packed and our canoe was lashed on top. There were folded blankets and boxes and paddles sticking out all over.

Indian Pete had just come back from a trip into the forests upstate and had brought a saddle of 'beef' with him. No one had to ask him what the meat really was. Miss Pauline knew exactly how to cook wild meat, which tends to be dry. I helped her while Pete and my father and Tim sat out on the porch talking. First we made sure to get all the tallow off, because that's what gives venison the strong taste most people don't like. I did that, stripping the yellowish fat from between the bulging chunks of muscle while Miss Pauline prepared the broth. She had cooked down some onions and beef gravy; when I was finished, she poured it over the deer meat until there was perhaps an inch or so of it in the bottom of the Dutch oven. Then she put the pot over the heat with the lid on. Soon we heard juices simmering, and a little cloud of steam rose from one corner where the lid was cracked.

'You peel the potatoes,' she said. 'We'll add them half an hour before everything else is done.'

'Yes ma'am,' I said, putting a dozen small potatoes in a bowl of water to soak. I didn't – and don't – like peeling potatoes, but if they are to be eaten, someone has to peel them. Miss Pauline smiled at me.

'You're a real help around the house,' she said.

'Thank you, ma'am.'

'You're going to make some boy a good wife,' as if that were the greatest compliment she could pay. I suppose it was.

I dug the knife into a potato to take out the eyes, wishing Miss Pauline wouldn't keep talking about boys and getting married. But she was wound up like the Edison player. She spent the next hour asking me if there was any special boy at school I liked and if any of the other girls were 'keeping company.' You may think that was strange, since I was only thirteen, but you must remember that in those days a girl married early, often at fifteen or sixteen, and she was an old maid at twenty. As I may have said, Miss Pauline seemed terribly old to me. There was grey in her hair, yet she was only thirty-one that year we took the canoe trip.

We added the potatoes and some carrots to the venison roast and went outside where it was cool. My father and Indian Pete were talking.

'Wait one week,' Pete was saying. 'I go with you.'

'I can't,' said my father. 'Hunting season starts the twenty-sixth, and I've got a party from Long Island.'

Pete frowned. 'No like. Suppose you get sick? Two young 'uns by themselves, what they do?'

My father smiled. 'Very well, I think. But I won't get sick. Why should I, on this trip of all trips? I wish you *could* go, Pete, but only because we'd have fun together. Can't you postpone your client?'

Pete shook his head. 'Him important man. World come to end if he don't get home to stock market.'

My father laughed. 'What's he paying you?'

'Heap wampum,' said Pete, straight-faced.

'Come on, noble savage. Don't beat around the bush.'

'Ten dollars a day,' said Pete. 'And I charge him two-fifty for the canoe. He brings his own grub, and Indian Pete eats good.'

My father whistled. The going rate for guides was five to six dollars a day. Even that was high in those times when ten dollars a week was a good wage for a working man.

'You must know where the body's hidden,' said my father.

'No,' said Pete. His voice was clear and free of any Indian accent. 'I just look the other way when he shoots a deer out of season.'

My father sniffed the fragrant air. 'Well,' he smiled, 'we're glad you did.'

'You no understand,' said Pete, putting on his Indian voice again. 'Client, him shoot deer, leave it. No can cut off horns, either, because they still in velvet. He shoot just to shoot.'

My father's lips tightened. 'Why?'

'He go moose hunting in Canada, want to be sure rifle shooting straight. Say targets no good, must try on live game.'

'I don't think I would like your client,' said my father.

'I don't like him either,' I said.

Indian Pete gave me a big smile. 'You good shot, Miss Elizabeth?'

'I can shoot the eye out of a mosquito at fifty paces,' I boasted.

'Lizzy!' warned my father.

'Well, I can hit a tin can,' I corrected.

'You remember skunk we trapped?' Pete asked.

'Yes.'

'No waste. Kill'um, skin'um.'

'I remember,' I said, 'and you didn't even want him.'

'Great Spirit give'um, no waste'um. Skin, eat, put bones back in ground. Corn grow next year.'

'Pete,' I said, 'sometimes you talk just like my father and me, and sometimes you talk like the old Indians in books. Why?'

'I like to keep in practice,' Pete said.

We had breakfast early, before sunrise. Miss Pauline had fried eggs and home-cured bacon, salty and hot, and biscuits with honey and butter she'd churned the night before. She sat at the table with us but did not eat. She busied herself pouring coffee for my father, and milk for Tim and me and asking us if we wanted any more.

'Pauline,' my father said, 'we aren't going to the South Pole. The canoe is almost loaded to the gunwales now. If I eat any more, we'll founder.'

'Well,' I said, 'they think the Admiral is going to make it to the South Pole. I heard it on the radio last night.'

The mellow-voiced man had told us about the great expedition. It seemed as if this time they would succeed in reaching the bottom of the world. He had told, also, of a terrible train wreck in Iowa and of a gang of convicts who had escaped from the jail in Glens Falls, probably over the border into Vermont.

'I wish Pete were going with you,' Miss Pauline said.

'So do I,' said my father. 'He's a good man in the woods. Maybe next time.' He stood up. 'Time to go. Is everything loaded?'

It had been my job to check each item off the list we had prepared. I could have done it from memory, but I

34

had used the list just to be safe. 'We didn't forget a thing,' I said.

'Well, if we did, we can do without it,' said my father. He kissed Miss Pauline and she let her hands cling to his back for a moment, then she busied herself clearing the table. She said without looking at Tim and me, 'You have a good time, and don't give your father any back talk, you hear me?'

We kissed her goodbye and rushed out to the car and crammed ourselves into the front seat beside father. The back seat was piled high with gear and supplies. My father retarded the spark, set the hand throttle on the steering-wheel, cranked the motor, leaped in to advance the spark, and away we went. The new state road wasn't finished then, but the dirt road to Blue Mountain Lake was open, and we rattled over it as the sun rose behind us, throwing the Model T's long shadow down the dusty hills ahead of us. There were no car radios in those days, a lack we made up for by singing at the top of our lungs. Tim was mauling 'There's a Long, Long Trail A-Winding', and nothing my father and I could sing would divert his attention from that song, so we finally threw down the towel and joined in with him. Then we sang 'Oh, How I Hate to Get Up in the Morning', and 'Casey Jones'.

It was still early when we reached Blue Mountain Lake, and the general store was still closed. Two horses were tied outside the bank, so someone must have been inside working – or robbing it. We stopped at a garage on the edge of town for a can of oil and a cold pop for Tim and me.

'Enjoy it,' warned my father. 'You won't see another bottle of pop for ten days.'

'Going camping?' asked the garage man.

'Yes,' my father said. 'I thought I'd show the kids the deer herds and maybe a moose before winter comes on. Looks to be a bad one this year.'

'It'll be that,' said the garage man. 'I saw three flocks

of Canadian geese going over last evening, and here it's not even November.'

'Well,' said my father, 'we're sure having an Indian summer now.'

'I hope it lasts for you,' said the garage man. 'You going up towards the Saranacs?'

'Tupper Lake,' my father said. 'Plan to canoe down Beaver Creek. It ought to run good. We may have to portage once or twice.'

The garage man whistled. 'Jiminy,' he said. 'Where can you put a canoe into Beaver Creek?'

'Well,' my father said, 'I was hunting up this way last year, and there was a pretty good logging road cutting in just above Cat Mountain. I thought we'd drive the Lizzie in as far as we could and then pack the rest of the way.'

'Jiminy,' the man said again. 'Wisht I was going with you. That sounds like the cat's pyjamas.'

'Maybe next time,' said my father. 'You fish?'

'Does a dog howl?' He laughed. 'Well, you be careful.'

'We will,' promised my father, and we drove away. I had finished drinking my pop, but I still had the bottle. I showed it to my father. 'We forgot to give the man back his bottle,' I said.

'We can let him have it when we come to pick up the car,' said my father. 'I guess the Coca-Cola company can trust him for a couple of bottles.'

We sang some more. My father taught us the words to 'The Erie Canal', and soon the woods were echoing to:

> Low bridge, everybody down!
> Low bridge, for we're going through a town,
> And you'll always know your neighbour,
> You'll always know your pal,
> If you've ever navigated on the Erie Canal!

We reached the vicinity of Cat Mountain around noon. It was off to our left, in the west, since we were driving north. My father began to look for the logging trail that led off to the east. Soon he found it, and we turned off the gravel road on to a rutted dirt trail. It was easy going, though slow, and cool under the trees. We stopped once and had some cold chicken which Miss Pauline had packed for us, and my father drank beer from a bottle with a cap that was clamped down like the rubber-washered top of a Mason jar. I didn't know where he had got the beer, because there was certainly none at home. I suppose he must have slipped it from the garage man at Blue Mountain Lake, which, now that I think on it, is probably the reason we stopped, as he never did use that can of oil he bought. Tim and I had some iced tea with sugar. As we ate, we speculated on what the kids in school were doing and whether they were envious of us. My father told us not to make fun of them when we returned, because, as he put it, playing hookey was against the letter, if not the spirit, of the law, and there was no point in rubbing it in. So we changed the subject and discussed the best way to train a bird dog. Tim held for letting him run wild and keep his kill, but I remembered having read somewhere that that would only make the dog resentful when he began hunting for men and had his catch taken away. My father intervened with a position that compromised between the two, and then we were on our way again and singing once more.

Last year, I rode with a neighbour from my home in Albany to Amsterdam, New York, where a manufacturer wanted to discuss some conservation litter bags for cars. She brought her two children who huddled in the back seat, chilled by the air conditioning, and played with printed games the gas station had given us. My neighbour had the radio turned up so loud that I could hardly hear the tyres against the highway although we were driving almost sixty. For the entire two hours I heard only the mumbling voice of a disc jockey and the blare of the records he played. How different it is today from that October morning when my father and Timmy and I drove slowly back into the Adirondacks, hearing the song of the birds and the whisper of the wind and even

37

the distant cry of a feeding loon.

Twice we had to stop and chop a path through fallen trees to give the Model T room to pass. Other than that, the trail was no problem. The high clearance of the Ford enabled it to step right over rocks and the hump between the ruts. We didn't drive fast, of course. Warm air flowed over the windshield, which •my father had lowered, bathing our faces with its many fragrances.

Both my father and Tim had watches. Timmy's was a cheap turnip which had originally belonged to my father, who gave it to him when he invested in his own, a gold Hamilton railroad watch with the numerals in Roman. Tim's kept fairly good time as long as he remembered to wind it, which was twice a day, but my father frequently bragged that his Hamilton was accurate down to a minute a month. On several occasions I have seen him prove it by comparisons against the Western Union clock at the railroad station.

When we reached the creek, Tim's turnip said it was five past three, while my father's Hamilton proclaimed that the hour was 3 : 11. Either way, we had a problem — and a hard decision to make. By the time we were unloaded, it would easily be 5.30, and daylight would start to fail around 7.30. Should we load up the canoe and proceed an hour or so downstream before setting up camp or should we set up camp here by the edge of the creek and waste that hour or so of travel time?

My father asked for our opinions. Tim was all for pressing on. I argued against him. 'We have had a long day already,' I pointed out, 'and we will be very tired before we set foot in the canoe. What can an hour of paddling gain us? Three or four miles downstream? Then we have to find a good camp and get it ready. Here we have a perfect camp. We can spend our time packing everything aboard the canoe that we won't need for sleeping or breakfast. That will give us an early start, which will more than make up for the hour we lose this evening.'

Tim grumbled, but my father cast his vote with me,

and we set about unloading the Ford. My father suggested that, since we now knew how to gather materials for a browse bed, we do so while he loaded the canoe. We fetched poles and balsam boughs and, although it pains me to admit it, Tim did a more than passable job in laying down the bed. I helped, toting and holding what he required, and before long we had constructed a bed that would have done Warren G. Harding proud.

Meanwhile my father had taken the canoe down carefully and slipped it into the water, where he tied it to two trees, fore and aft. Then he began to sort our gear. That which was not needed for our overnight camp was piled on the bank near the canoe and covered with the canvas fly.

'We won't need the fly tonight,' he said. 'The sky is clear and the wind is from the north.'

'Why should that make a difference?' I asked.

'I'm not sure,' he said. 'But I've noticed that when rain arrives, it almost always comes from the south or the southwest. If the wind is from the northwest or the north, it will nearly always be cool and dry.'

'One day,' I declared, 'weather men will take that into account. Maybe they will be able to predict the weather more than five minutes in advance.'

My father laughed and gave me the finger against the side of his nose, indicating that I was 'blue skying' again.

My father was right that evening of October 15th. It did not rain but became quite cool. We were grateful for the warm camp fire he had built in a semicircle of large stones.

Our supper was to be fried rabbit and boiled potatoes. We had just finished making our browse bed and the sun was touching the tops of the pines when my father turned to Tim and said: 'Is your rifle ready?'

'Yes,' Tim said. He touched his pockets. 'I have some shells right here.'

'Then take it and walk up the trail slowly. I think you'll see something for our supper.'

Tim didn't question my father but quietly took his

39

rifle from the Model T and, pointing the muzzle away from us, slipped a .22 cartridge into its breech. He didn't cock the hammer, but instead put on the safety, which brought a nod of approval from my father. Tim slipped quietly up the trail and disappeared around the bend.

'Did you see some game?' I asked.

'This forest is alive with game. It's only necessary to keep your eye peeled.'

I heard the sharp report of Tim's rifle. My father smiled. 'I think we'd better get the frying-pan ready,' he said.

'Maybe he missed,' I said.

'I don't think so,' said my father. 'Your brother is a very good shot.'

'He may be that,' I agreed, 'but he'll never be my brother.'

My father frowned. 'Don't say such things. Tim lives in the same house and eats the same food and loves you as truly as any natural brother.'

'I agree,' I said. 'And although I would never allow him to hear it from me, I love Tim too. But he's my stepbrother. There's no blood between us.'

'I hope you've never said this to him.'

'Of course I never have. Anything I have or can get is his for the asking. But I must be honest with myself.'

My father shook his head and mumbled something I didn't catch. Before I could ask him to repeat it, there came another shot.

'You see?' I cried. 'He missed the first time.'

My father didn't answer but began unpacking the cooking gear and organizing it on the front fender of the Model T. Soon Tim came around the bend, carrying three small rabbits by the hind legs. I stared at them and said: 'How did you get three rabbits with only two shots?'

'I saw two in line,' he said proudly. 'I squatted down and shot right through the first one and hit the second. Then I got number three with the other shot.'

'Good boy,' said my father. 'Lizzy, you get the potatoes

started. Tim and I will clean these babies.'

I got some water from the creek and began peeling potatoes, which I didn't mind today. Anything was better than skinning rabbits.

'Let me show you an easy way to clean a rabbit out,' my father said. 'You don't even need a knife.'

I watched as he dug his fingers under the rib cage of one of the rabbits and tore open the hide to reveal the entrails. Then he held the front feet in his hand and bent the carcass backwards so that he had the rear feet held in the same hand too, and the rabbit was bent like a horse-shoe. As if he were throwing a stick, my father snapped the rabbit forward but didn't let go. It remained in his hand, but all the innards went flying out into the woods.

'Clean as a whistle,' my father said, showing Tim the glistening cavity. 'Now here's how you finish skinning him.' He poked a stick through a loose fold of hide on the rabbit's back, opened up a fingergrip which he took with both hands. Then he snapped his hands apart, and the hide peeled back like two pairs of gloves and the rabbit was bare meat, with the hide attached only at the feet. He snapped the little legs and the hide came free. He had a completely dressed rabbit ready for the pot.

'All right,' said my father, 'you do the other two, and I'll get the fire going.'

He tore some curls of birchbark from a nearby tree and piled them inside a small circle of stones, heaping twigs on top. Then he broke some larger dead branches and added them to the heap, struck a match, and in no time had a cheerful fire blazing away.

I finished the potatoes and put fresh water in the pot, then propped it up on two of the stones so that the fire struck it. One of the tin plates made a satisfactory lid to keep the heat in and the ashes out.

An hour later we were stretched out, enjoying the last red glow of the sun and picking our teeth. Three small rabbits do not go far with so many hungry people in the woods, and the potatoes had vanished too. My father had rolled the rabbit meat in a little flour, heavily seasoned with salt and pepper, and then fried it to a crisp brown over the camp fire. The crowned heads of Europe had never eaten anything more delicious. To me, tender young rabbit is tastier than the finest chicken white meat.

My father's pipe gave the air a nice warm smell that mixed with the sharper tang of the pine scent. I remember him and Tim talking about the way to tell that a rabbit is free of liver flukes, and that's all I remember, because the long day and the satisfaction of the meal and the warm glow of the camp fire sent me right off to sleep.

Dawn found us awake and raring to go. We made a hasty breakfast of cold biscuits from the package Miss Pauline had given us and started loading the canoe.

First my father put four light spruce poles in the bottom. 'That'll keep the gear out of any water we may take over the side,' he explained, starting to pile the gear along the centre line of the canoe. He put all the heavy stuff down in the bottom, including some canned goods, and then covered them with the canvas fly and began piling our sleeping-blankets and extra clothing on it. He tied it all up by folding the canvas over and fastening it with a bit of heavy twine.

'All right, Miss Lizzy,' he told me. 'You get up in the bow, facing back. Roll your jacket up and use it as a rest. Otherwise that thwart will leave its mark on your back.'

I stepped carefully into the canoe, putting my weight in its centre as I had been taught, and lowered myself down to my position. Then Tim boarded. He sat in the centre, on a small bit of folded canvas. The load of supplies was directly behind him. My father pushed the canoe out into the water and got in carefully, balancing on his knees just in front of the rear thwart.

So, just a few minutes after sunrise, we slid silently down the brown, muddy waters of the creek. Our great adventure had begun.

No one who has ever boiled up a stream propelled by a noisy, smelly outboard motor will ever know how peaceful yet exciting an hour on the water can be. Only the silent canoe is accepted by nature as one of her own and permitted to join in the normal rhythms and flow of riverbank life. Within a half mile, which took only a few minutes paddling downstream, we had seen a good dozen muskrats. Because of the canoe's shallow draft, we skimmed over water that would defy other boats. From my 'parlour chair' in the bow of the canoe I could see all that passed. I enjoyed watching my father and Tim at their paddling – which, thanks to the downstream flow of our creek, wasn't strenuous.

The paddles were hand-carved. I remember the winter my father shaped them, sitting in front of the fire while the snow howled outside, whittling slowly and steadily at two large pieces of maple. He talked as he worked, not so much because he thought I would remember or understand what he said but merely to fill the quiet hours.

'I'll make these paddles with a squared-off bottom edge,' he said. 'Those seem to hold up better than the Maine guide or the beavertail, which are rounded and tend to smash up on a rocky bottom.'

'That's nice, Father,' I replied, not knowing if I were agreeing to fish or fowl. But now in the creek, I could watch as the long paddles dipped into the brown water and see what my father had described. The maple wood was naturally springy. It let the paddlers get a good bite in the water without digging in as if they were trying to dig a ditch. We carried a spare paddle lashed to the side of the canoe, but it was one of the heavy clumsy ones Pete had given us when he brought my father the canoe. Nor were my father's paddles painted. 'Paint only covers up a flaw someone's trying to hide,' he told me as he protected the maple with several thin coats of varnish. He pointed out that he was not varnishing the handle, where it would be gripped by the hand. 'Blisters come soon enough on a long day,' he said. 'No point in adding varnish to help them along. Skin oil worked into the wood will protect it well enough.'

I watched them at their rowing. My father sat loosely,

rolling with the motion of the canoe. His right hand was clasped over the grip while the other held the shaft loosely, with his arm out straight. He matched movements with Tim's. Although each time Tim's paddle bit into the water, I felt the canoe try to surge to that side, my father twisted his paddle, which put us back on the straight and narrow.

The water was deep, and we did not have to jig sideways to avoid rocks or sunken trees. The hours floated by. There was a light breeze, so the bugs didn't pester us. All we needed was a freezer can of ice-cream and a brass band and it would have been like the Fourth of July. I even dozed awhile.

'Look.'

I tilted my head up and caught sight of a flock of ducks going over. They seemed close.

'We'll have rain soon,' said my father.

'How do you know?' I asked.

'Those ducks were too low for the middle of the day. They're looking for shelter. We'd better do the same or we'll soon be wet.'

The breeze seemed fresher. There was that musty, cold smell in the air that often precedes a rainstorm. I concluded that he was right and began to look around for a convenient landing-spot.

Tim saw one first – a long, sloping bank along the edge of the creek. Spruce trees grew down almost to the edge of the water. They would help shield us from the rain. Tim and my father pulled for it. We had just gone ashore when the first of the rain hit. We took the bit of folded canvas Tim had been using for a seat and spread it over some branches and sat down beneath it, snug and cosy. It was almost noon, so we ate the last scraps of the food Miss Pauline had provided for us – more cold biscuits, some fried chicken, and a soggy chunk of blueberry pie. Now we would be on our own as far as food went, except for the beans and a few other cans we had brought along.

When we had finished my father said quietly: 'I've made a mistake.'

44

'What do you mean?' Tim said.

'I've been watching the sun. We're not in Beaver Creek. I must have taken the wrong logging trail off the main road. Beaver Creek heads steadily northwest. We've been working our way east.'

'I'll get the map,' Tim said.

'No, never mind. I'll show you later where we are. But it is my opinion that we have gotten ourselves into one of the tributaries of Cold River. That means that if we continue our course, we'll find ourselves on the way to Schoon Lake or even Pottersville. I don't think we could go as far as Ticonderoga, although it might be possible. Now we have a decision to make. Should we work back upstream and take the canoe to the right logging trail, so as to continue our original plan, or should we change our minds and make Pottersville our destination?'

Slowly Tim said: 'If we stay in the Cold River, will we still see the wild game you promised?'

'I think so,' my father said.

'How long would it take to get back to the Model T?' I asked.

'At least a full day, maybe more,' said my father. 'But remember, if we stay in the Cold River, no one will know where to look for us if we turn up overdue.'

'That doesn't bother me,' I said. 'I'm against retracing our trail. That's only wasted motion. It doesn't matter which river we ride as long as we're not lost.' How easily I said the words – and how much, later, I wished I never had.

'I think Lizzy's right,' said Tim.

'Okay,' said my father. 'I don't know how I made such a dumb mistake, but we'll just do our best with it.'

The brief rain shower was over, so we reboarded the canoe, bailed water for a few minutes, and continued our journey.

As the long afternoon lazed around us, I began trailing a line overboard with a grasshopper on the hook. I had tied a small stone a foot or so above the bait, so that the hopper was either on the surface or just a foot or so beneath the water. It was not more than ten minutes until there was a disturbed circle of water around where the line vanished into the depths. Then I felt the solid pull of a fish on the line. I gave it a sturdy yank to set the hook and then brought in the line, hand over hand. My catch was a nice brook trout, easily two pounds. I flopped him into the boat and pried the hook out of his mouth. The grasshopper was still attached, so I had bait for the next try. I rigged a stringer from an extra bit of line and put it through the trout's gills so he could swim around the canoe while I explored for his brothers. During the day I added three more trout and a dark monster that my father identified as a small-mouthed bass to the string.

The sun was low as we began to search for a camp site. As we did, my father said, 'Miss Lizzy, since you're the camp chef today, you can clean your catch.'

I protested but to no avail. Tim passed me his pocket knife, and my father said: 'You'll have no trouble with the trout. Just stick your knife into their vents and cut a slit up to the bottom of their jaws.' I did so, then he instructed: 'Now take your finger and run it up the inside of the backbone and scoop out the innards.' The prospect repelled me, but I did as he said. When I reached the bright red gills, my father said: 'Now snap them towards the top of his head.' I did and everything popped out neatly. The second was easier, and the third needed no prompting at all. By the last, I was an expert. The bass needed scaling first. I did that with the short blade of Tim's knife, which was dull, getting almost as many of the glistening scales on my legs as I did over the side. I was so occupied that I did not notice that my father had located a camp site. Just as I finished gutting the bass, we shuddered ashore, the canvas making a sandpaper sound on the bank. My father held the canoe steady while we got out. As I rinsed the fish in the running water, he and Tim began unloading.

This time we made a proper camp, with the big canvas fly overhead and everything unpacked and distributed

46

according to purpose. I smiled as Tim drew the chore of peeling the potatoes, while I helped lay and start the camp-fire. My father produced a surprise from inside his pack — a mixture of vanilla and sugar which, when combined with cold water from the creek, formed a brew almost as tasty as the pop we had enjoyed at the Blue Mountain Lake garage. When everything was ready to eat — the fish floured and salt and peppered, the potatoes soft and steaming, and the coffee fragrant in the blackened pot — my father allowed Tim and me to have half a cup each of coffee, weakened by almost as much condensed milk from a can.

It was a fine meal. For dessert we had little squares of maple candy which had also appeared miraculously from my father's private pack. He had been thinking specially of us when he prepared this trip. I lay on my comfortable blanket, cradled by the softness of the thatched spruce branches, and watched him near the fire, his jaw lean and shadowed by the dancing flames. He was smoking his pipe. Even now, when I remember my father, that is how I see him.

The stars were bright through the trees. I could see the Little and Big Dippers, and the Seven Sisters, and the Milky Way. We talked quietly of many things — of the second cow we hoped to get next spring, of the rumour that soon there would be a new school in which each grade would have its own room, of Tim's hope to run his own trap line for extra money that winter. There was nothing of great importance that we said, but all that we spoke was close and dear to us, and there was no inter-rupting outside voice such as a television set or stereo record player to distract us.

Tim cried: 'What was that?' pointing at the sky. I sat up and stared. For a moment I saw nothing, then I saw a swift streak of light move rapidly across the patch of darkness.

'A falling star!' I said.

My father nodded. 'Yes,' he said, 'this batch usually comes around the middle of October.'

'How can that be?' I asked. I knew what a falling star

was, but I had never heard of *showers* of them at that time, and I don't think my father had either. Yet with a woodsman's observations, he knew that the Orionids, which were the ones we were seeing now, always came in mid-October, and that the Deminids would come in December, and that in April you could count on the Lyrids. He knew neither their names nor their origins, but had come to accept and expect them at their appointed times.

'Maybe,' he promised, 'I'll show you something even prettier in the morning – if you don't mind getting up early.'

'What, Father?' I asked. But instead of giving in, he put his finger beside his nose and smiled.

How prodigal we are with that which is so precious! If only I could have captured and preserved that smile! But no, we downgrade and misplace that which is easily come by, recognizing its value only when it is too late. So I carelessly let one of my father's last smiles waste itself against my smug indifference and sank into sleep, blissfully supposing that there were a million more where that one came from.

A touch awoke me. The fire was dim, burned down to glowing coals, and dawn was only a promise in the eastern sky.

'What?'

My father said, 'Shhh, Lizzy. Come and look.'

I rubbed the sleep from my eyes. Tim was already up, standing near the fire, peering up into the sky.

I joined him and gasped. 'What is it? Are the woods on fire?'

'I've never seen them so bright,' said my father, pointing.

I stared. The northern sky was filled with arcs and streamers of light, all green and red and yellow. They radiated from the horizon like a great fan, pulsing like the neon gas tubes we had seen outside certain road-houses on the state highway.

'What are they?' I asked.

'The northern lights,' my father said. 'We're lucky. Most times they're just a dull glow in the sky.'

Fascinated, I said: 'Why don't we see them at home?'

With a chuckle in his voice, he said, 'They're at their brightest just before dawn. Have you ever gotten up to look?'

Shamed, I admitted, 'No.'

Tim said, 'They make you feel mighty small.'

My father answered: 'No, Tim. Rather, when you are alone in the woods and see their glowing fingers, they always remind you that God is everywhere and that there is no darkness deep enough to make you afraid.'

We were silent. The aerial display was enough to make you hold your breath. Then as we watched, the lights flickered, faded, and were gone.

'All right,' said my father, 'back to bed. It's only 4.00 a.m. We have a couple of hours yet till dawn.'

I crawled into my share of the browse bed, but it was a long time before I went back to sleep.

The sun was barely over the edge of the trees, but we had been on the river for two hours. We were ready at dawn. No one slept much after the display of the northern lights. My father was up feeding the fire and cooking breakfast before it was truly light.

Tim and I joined him as soon as the fire took the chill out of the air. We had lain awhile in the bed, whispering about the northern lights. Neither of us had ever been so awed before, not even when Arnie Lindstrom took a 46-pound catfish out of North Creek.

'Maybe God *is* up there,' Tim said. He and I had been arguing recently about the existence of God. Tim was willing to believe on the basis that it did no harm, and that if there was a God, He would be fooled. I disagreed, because to me the world was simply too complicated to have merely happened. Tim posed such hard-to-answer questions as, If there is an all-seeing God, why did he permit the Great War to occur, killing and maiming

49

millions of innocents? I was armed with quotations from the Bible, since, having read quite a bit of it, I knew almost every word. But none of them seemed to answer a *real* question, I guess because it was hard to imagine ourselves riding asses and wearing sandals as we went through life, like those Israelites did.

So I tried to use common sense, which when dealing with Tim can sometimes be a mistake. After I completed all my explanations, Tim merely put his finger up to his nose, copying my father, and declared that I knew no more than he did, and that, like him, I was coppering my bet just in case there *was* a God who might call me to account later on for not believing. Yet in case I have not said so, there has never been a boy I knew who was more gentle or compassionate towards living creatures than Tim. He would step over a bug and would agonize for days over an injured calf or a mangey dog. That didn't keep him from shooting game for the pot, for it was well understood that the life of the woods was subordinate to the needs of men. But if ever a speck of cruelty invaded the thoughts of Timothy Hood, I never knew of it.

Our progress down the river – or creek, for we were not yet in the main stream of the Cold River – was silent. I let my hand drag over the side, but the water was cold, so I took it out and dried it off. I was wearing boy's Levi jeans, which suited me although Miss Pauline always had a fit when I wore them to town. My heavy wool shirt was soft and warm. No bug in a rug could have been snugger.

The first sign that something was unusual came when my father feathered his paddle in the water, slowing the canoe and turning it to one side. He made a little 'shhh' sound, hardly louder than the sigh of the breeze, and nodded his head to one side. I looked, and my heart leaped.

At the edge of the stream, drinking, were two does and four fawns. The does were large, deep-bodied, and rich brown. The fawns had lost their spots, but they were still pale. With their large, flicking ears and big black noses, they looked like cheerful little calico toys.

My father and Tim backed water and put the canoe into a little cove where we sat holding our breaths and watching the deer. Soon they were joined by several others, including one big buck whose horns were at least two feet over and in front of his head. They looked odd, as if moss were dropping from them.

My father whispered: 'He's just coming out of velvet. He's been rubbing his horns on trees to take off the skin.'

'He's beautiful,' I whispered.

'There hasn't been much hunting around here,' my father said. 'A buck will reach his full growth of horns in three or four years if he isn't bothered. Then he'll start to fall off until when he's an old grey-head, he may be just a spike-horn again like the first-year stags.'

'Do the does always have twins?' I asked.

'More often than not,' my father said. 'Those fawns over there were born just a couple of months ago. It's too bad, but they'll never make it through to spring if I'm right about this winter.'

'It doesn't seem fair. They've just been born.'

'Nature is cruel,' he said. 'The bucks will wear themselves out, running around servicing the does during rut. Bucks die first, because they're weak and frazzled. A doe will try to help her young, but when the browse gets low, the fawns won't be able to reach up far enough. There's no nourishment in bark, and they'll go next. Funny as it seems, it's the weak female does that usually survive the winter – although not many of them will make it this year either.'

He reached for his rifle, then drew back.

I said, 'You weren't going to shoot one of them, were you?'

'Yes, Lizzy,' he said sternly. 'I was. Later in the trip, if the weather cools, I will. You've got to be hard in your heart. Not one in ten over there will live past March. Better they should fill our bellies than rot under the snow.'

'But,' I asked, 'how will you know that you aren't shooting the one in ten that would have lived?'

My point was a telling one, for he didn't answer.

We watched the deer as they drank and then slowly moved up the bank. I don't believe, despite their vaunted reputation for keen senses, that any one of them was aware of our presence. It's too bad that in those days we didn't have Super 8 movie cameras with all their lenses and gadgets for capturing for ever what happened long ago. I know that your eyes would soften and your breath would catch if you were able to see those lovely brown creatures sipping delicately at the refreshing edge of the stream, their lustrous black eyes roving the hills and ravines in search of danger. Near Albany, I have often taken friends to certain glens and dells I know where deer can be seen, although these days we need ten-power field glasses to see their faces. There must be primitive reaction to deer within people, unknowing and unsquared with their 'civilization', just as there is to the sea. I suppose the difference is between the people today and those of 1921. Then we could love the deer and enjoy watching them, and still put them into the pot and enjoy their meat, while folks today choke on wild meat.

'When I was a boy,' said my father, 'we had herds of deer bigger than that come right up behind the cabin and graze on our potato plants.'

To me, that seemed an eternity. 'Was that before the Civil War?' My father laughed, and the sound startled those deer remaining. They ran up the bank and were gone.

As we proceeded, the stream became faster. Now there were occasional rocks to avoid, with white foam flecked around their upstream surfaces. My father warned us to keep a sharp lookout for underwater dangers and snags.

Disaster, when it came, was sudden and unexpected.

We turned a curve in the stream, and all was tranquil and laughing, for my father had just finished chastising Tim for catching a 'crab' with his paddle. Then we were suddenly in a raceway of white water and black, forbidding stones. My father yelled: 'Tim, paddle with all your might! Lizzy, take the extra paddle and face front. Push off any stones you see. I'll steer. Call out the channel.'

My heart sank. I had never 'called out the channel' before except in a rowboat while stalking frogs on a summer evening. But there was no choice now, so I scanned the water ahead and watched like a hawk for dangers beneath the surface.

We were racing downstream now like a four-horse rig on its way to the fair. The channel seemed clear, so I kept silent. My father was busy shouting to Tim – 'Paddle right! Paddle left!' The canoe kept right end to, however. While there was a slight element of fear, I was thrilled and laughing each time we shot past a threatening outcropping of rock.

Then the channel narrowed, and I began to shout: 'Rocks on the right! Look out ahead!' Tim stroked as hard as he could to give us steerageway, and my father, perched high up on the stern of the canoe, watched and steered our fragile vessel between the stone walls of the rampaging stream. They shot past us like the bridge supports when we'd taken a train to Albany, white blurs caught only in the corner of the eye. From far in front I heard an even more frightening sound – *the roar of white water*. 'Rapids ahead!' I shouted, but it was no use. There was no way we could avoid them. We sped between the ever-higher walls. Now the waves that backed up behind some of the underwater reefs cascaded into the canoe, drenching me along the way. I held my paddle ready, and once had to jam it against a floating tree trunk that threatened to capsize us. The impact numbed my hands, and it was all I could do to hang on to the paddle.

'Paddle right!' my father shouted to Tim, and the canoe sluiced to one side, barely missing an underwater ridge I hadn't seen. There was no word of reproach, but I knew I had failed and had almost scuttled our fragile craft. Guilt rose in me like seasickness.

We shot around a curve, and what we saw made us freeze with fear. Downstream boiled a cloud of white spray from a narrow raceway of water that was more a waterfall than rapids. We were headed straight for it. Now my father's voice was snatched away by the wind as he cried, 'Lizzy! Fend off!' I had more than I could do for the next few moments, jamming my paddle down to shove us away from the rocks. I soon learned to brace it against the bow of the canoe, but even then the shock of the impact was enough to make my wrists ache. There was no more laughter now as we cascaded towards the bottom of that incredible flume, but rather fear and dread, because we could see that at the end of the raceway was a tumble of surf and a whirling eddy that was such a boiling churn of white water that there was no liquid visible at all – only spray and foam.

It was too late to save ourselves. We plunged into foaming, watery chaos, water brimming over some unseen dropoff. We fell down its yielding side like a bobsled. When we hit the wave of water at the bottom, it was as ungiving as a wall of ice.

The canoe shot into the air. As it turned over, I remember thinking: *But I'm not ready to die!* It seemed as if I floated in the air for hours, but still there was no time to take a breath and so store up more time to live beneath the black waters.

Then time came back to life as I was plunged into the icy water. Suddenly I was strangling. A voice spoke inside my head, telling me to be calm and hold my breath, but as the rocky bottom scraped my back, I gasped without meaning to, and some water got into my throat. I coughed it out and, with an effort more resolute than any I had ever made, refrained from trying to breath. My chest burned. It was an exquisite agony.

To my amazement, my head shot out of the water, and I had time to gasp a quick breath before I was thrown under again. I tried to look about in that brief time, to see where my father or Tim or the canoe was, but to no avail. Under the raging stream once more, I began to have a faint hope that I might survive if I used my head. I opened my eyes and in blurred fishy fashion fended myself away from threatening rocks and the sunken trees that lined the bottom. It seemed that I could *hear* the stones grinding under the liquid torrent. I prayed that I would be thrown to the surface soon, for my resolve not to breathe until my head had broken out beneath the sky was fast weakening. My prayer was answered. I was heaved once more to the surface and this time was able to suck in two breaths before being drawn under again.

At no time was I convinced that I would survive. I felt, as I did with the deer on the river bank, that it was a shame one so young should perish, but there was no real hope that the Almighty would see things my way and remit his dreadful verdict. It was truly as if I were trapped in a senseless maze, the kind one finds in Sunday colour supplements. If the pencil of my fate traced the proper route, I would find salvation; while if it faltered, I would go down to a watery death. Neither prospect pleased or disturbed me, for such definitions were not part of the wet, tumbling world in which I existed.

Perhaps my ancestors long ago had been caught in such cascades, for it was as if a voice spoke to me of my plight, informing me that, while I was still caught in the swirl of the stream's overflow, I was also being carried ever downstream through the undertow and that as I was tumbled along the bottom, I would be thrown up to the daylight and life again if I could only endure. The voice spoke true, for I was. Again I gasped at the nourishing air and then plunged, unresisting, into the depths once more. But each cycle of water – bottom and air – was weaker. Finally the moment came when I could remain afloat and try to reach the shore. By then I was so weak, so bruised, so despairing, that I was quite ready to die, except for the fact that the overturned canoe came to my hand and I caught it by one side and kicked out with my legs and propelled it towards the dim grey haze that I knew to be the distant bank.

At one time, I think (for I can't remember exactly what I felt on that long-ago day), I had wished for death to end the agony in my lungs. But now it was just the opposite. I cried out for life, now that there was time for a second breath, and even a third. To breathe without pain was a delight I had forgotten. But with this delight came another evil. I was so tired that the thought of sleep was a delicious promise I would have given all to collect. But I was able to resist its siren call and guide the overturned canoe into an eddy where I pulled it up on to the bank and collapsed, choking and puking. I wish I could say that I immediately hauled myself up a tree to search for my lost father and stepbrother, but I didn't. I was so sick that it was all I could do to summon enough energy to rid myself of the inhalations of the stream I had sucked down into my lungs.

I was aroused by a voice shouting, almost in my ear, 'Lizzy! Are you all right?'

I heaved myself to one elbow and saw my father, his clothing tattered and dripping, coming out of the bushes.

'I think so,' I gasped.

'Have you seen Tim?'

'No,' I said. 'Oh, Father, you're hurt!'

'It's just a stone bruise,' he said, touching his leg where it was purple and red. I knew even then that he was only trying to jolly me along, for it was obvious that his leg was broken beneath the knee. A bit of bone protruded from the skin, and blood dripped down his ankle. I got to him as quickly as I could and tore off my shirt. 'Give me your knife,' I ordered, and it is a measure of the confusion and pain in which he found himself, for he accepted my orders the same as he would have from another adult. I tore a strip from my shirttail and tied it around his leg, using a broken stick as a temporary splint to keep his leg from crumpling under him.

He winced as I cinched the knots but didn't complain. He drew in his breath in a shuddering gasp and said: 'Lizzy, we must find your brother.'

'You stay put,' I said. 'I'll find him.'

'He may need more help than you can give,' he said.

'If so, I'll call for help. Please – your leg is broken. If you move on it, it'll only get worse.'

It was evidence of his weakened state that he only touched my cheek and whispered, 'Hurry, Lizzy!'

I set off downstream, wading in the shallow water along the bank. I called, 'Tim? Tim? Answer me!' But I heard nothing.

It was hard going. I remember how easily I had answered my father when he asked me what to do if I got lost. The truth is, you're lucky to make two or three miles a day with such soggy going.

'Tim! Where are you?'

There was no answer. I was the smallest and lightest of the three, and I had come off with only a water-logged stomach. My father's leg was broken, and he had been in the best position of the canoe, in the rear, where it would not have struck him when it turned over. What could have happened to Tim, caught in the middle, as it shot into the air?

I never would have seen him, except that he had caught the floating, canvas-wrapped pack and dragged it to shore with him. He was collapsed over it, unconscious. All I saw was the brown lump of the pack, which is what kept me from walking past him.

I rushed over and shook his shoulder. 'Tim! Tim!'

He moved his head, so he was alive. I threw water in his face. Perhaps, after where he had been, he needed no more water, but at least he moved.

'Lizzy,' he gasped, 'is it you?'

'Do you hurt anywhere?'

He touched his legs, his arms, his belly. 'Yes,' he said. 'I hurt everywhere. But I don't think anything is broken.' He sat up, his eyes wide. 'Where's Dad?'

'His leg is broken. Come on, Tim, get up. We must make a fire and get dry.'

He struggled up. 'Help me carry this pack,' he said. 'I don't know what happened to the canoe.'

'It's safe. I pulled it ashore.'

'Then we're all right. We lost only the guns and the gear.'

'Don't forget father's broken leg.'

'Lizzy,' he said, sitting down. 'Lizzy, wait a minute, please.'

57

'What is it, Tim?'

He covered his face and began to cry.

'Oh, Tim,' I said. 'There's nothing to fear now. We're all safe.'

'I know,' he choked. 'Maybe that's why I'm crying.'

'Well, you can cry later. We've got to get back to Father and get a fire going.'

I helped him carry the pack. We found father sitting against a tree, his face white and his forehead covered with sweat. He tried to get up, but it was too much for him, and he slid down the tree trunk again, gasping.

'Don't move,' I called. 'Tim is all right. And we found the pack.'

His voice shaky, my father said: 'You'd better start a fire.'

'We will.' I began to pile some stones, and Tim was able to bring wood, although he moved slowly.

My father gave us a pack of the waxed matches from his pocket, and got the first one to light. Soon there was a warm fire blazing inside the pile of stones.

We sat close to it. Once my father had been warmed, his face took on some of its normal colour again. I took spare clothes out of the pack. They were damp but soon dried spread over a rope Tim had tied over the fire. We helped my father change his shirt, and Tim and I got into dry things too.

My father examined his leg. 'You did a good job under the circumstances, Miss Lizzy,' he said, 'but I think we had better get a larger splint. Is the camp axe safe?'

'Yes,' said Tim.

'Well,' my father said, 'we need a sturdy branch about two and a half feet long. You must pad it well with cloth so it will not be rough against the skin.' As Tim set out on that chore, my father went on, 'Lizzy, there is a bar of brown soap somewhere in the pack. Take it and a soft cloth, and we'll clean out any dirt we find in the wound.'

I located the soap, and rubbed it on a wet cloth and gave it to him. Wincing, he applied it to the raw edges where a bit of splintered bone protruded through his leg.

When Tim came back with the wood for a splint, I turned away while my father and Tim tied it on. I heard my father groan once with the pain, and the sound shot through me like a knife.

'All right,' he said. 'I'll be all right here near the fire. You two search for the paddles. But be careful, don't fall in the water again.'

We left him and worked our way down the creek bank. We went at least a mile but found no trace of the three paddles we had been using only an hour before. When we reported our failure to my father, he shook his head. 'We'll have to carve one,' he said. 'We can't go any farther without at least one paddle.'

'They may have floated up on the other side,' said Tim.

'Then they're lost,' my father told him. 'Lizzy, you had better put some beans to soaking, because they're all we'll have for supper. While you're in the pack, hand me my revolver. You never know, a rabbit might just come out into sight.'

'I could hunt for one,' said Tim.

'The rifles are gone,' said my father. 'And few men are a good enough pistol shot to hit a rabbit.'

'I saw a partridge while I was cutting the splint,' Tim said.

'Next time you see one, try to hit it with a stone,' said my father.

'I'll go look again,' said Tim.

'While you're in the woods, find a small birch tree,' my father said. 'The inner bark is sweet and good food. Cut several long strips, and we'll add them to the beans. Lizzy, while your brother is hunting, go down to the shore and examine the waterline. There may be fresh-water clams or crayfish that we can add to the supplies. We must use all the daylight we have. Later, when it's dark, we'll talk and make our plans.'

Tim went in one direction, while I did as my father had asked. I didn't see any clams, but I found several snails and one small green turtle. I didn't know what to do with them, but my father told me.

'Put the large pot near the fire,' he said. 'Get the water boiling, and then throw in the snails and the turtle.'

'But, Father,' I protested, 'they're still alive.'

He held out his hand and I put the turtle into it. He tried to cut its head off with his knife, but it withdrew into the shell. He placed the turtle on the ground. I stared in fascination as he struck its shell squarely in the centre with the butt of his revolver.

'Now it's dead,' he told me. 'If you can cut the head off, fine. Otherwise, hit the shell with something heavy. The concussion will kill it. Once the turtle is cooked, it'll be easy to quarter the underpart and scoop out the innards.' I put the turtle, which was oozing a green liquid, into the pot. When my father threw in the snails, I didn't say anything.

'I saw some pigweed near the water,' I said. 'Isn't that good to eat too?'

My father smiled weakly. 'Yes,' he said, 'particularly when you call it wild spinach rather than 'pigweed.' But there's no need for it just now. What we need are foods with fat or sugar in them. The turtle will help our rations considerably.'

He took out his Hamilton, but of course it was filled with water and ruined. Sadly he put it back in his pocket and squinted up through the trees. 'I'd say it is around two or three o'clock,' he said. 'There's no hope of our going on today. I have to carve a paddle before we can move, Lizzy, you'd better take the camp axe and cut branches for a browse bed.'

I jumped up. How stiff and uncomfortable he must have been lying on the bare ground!

By the time I finished that chore, the water was boiling and, at my father's request, I scooped up the turtle with two sticks and gave the steaming shell to him to clean out. The meat was cooked. To my surprise, it smelled like beef. Somehow I had thought turtle flesh would smell like fish.

Then he slid the snails out of their shells and tossed the dirty water away. I refilled the pot. Then, along with the bits of meat, I added a double handful of soaked

60

pinto beans and a pinch of soggy salt. My father watched me with interest.

'Is it true, darling,' he said, 'that you remember all you hear?'

'I can remember the words,' I said. 'As Miss Pauline said, sometimes I don't understand them.'

He sighed. I couldn't tell what was going through his mind.

The blankets were damp too, but when I wrapped one around his shoulders it steamed in the heat of the fire, and he seemed to be comfortable enough.

Once, half asleep, he looked up and cried, 'Damn it! Pete, I was a fool!'

I held his hand, which seemed to soothe him. He slept for about a half hour. By now I was concerned about Tim who had been gone far too long. I wanted to call him, but that would have disturbed my father.

When I was sure he was sleeping soundly, I went down and examined the canoe. It had sprung some small leaks but didn't seem badly damaged otherwise. I pulled it farther up on to the shore.

It was at that moment that I looked up and gasped. Someone had moved on the far bank of the creek. It was Tim. He saw me and waved, then held up something, and my heart leaped. It was one of the paddles! I wanted to call out but instead pointed at the fire and my sleeping father.

Tim waved again and disappeared in the woods. Since it was silly to stand around doing nothing, I set myself to sorting out the gear we had left and drying what was wet. We still had two pots, the big waxed block of matches, the knives and forks, and the dried beans. Two blankets had gone downstream, but there were two left. We still had some heavy fishing twine and a small box of hooks and some salt. My father had his revolver, but the hunting rifle and Tim's .22 had been lost. I searched inside every pocket of the few clothes we had remaining, but there was no sign of the map.

I heard a whistle from the woods and looked up in

time to see Tim appearing. In addition to the paddle, he carried two half-grown grey partridges. He was grinning.

'I didn't have any luck hitting them with rocks,' he said. 'But once I found the paddle, it was easy to hit them in the neck with the blade. They didn't seem to have any fear of people this far in the woods.'

'How did you get on the other side of the creek?' I asked. 'Father didn't want us to go over there.'

'I found a shallow place and waded across. From the way the water ran, it seemed that at least one of the paddles ought to have been there – and it was.'

He bent over and sniffed at the pot. 'Smells good,' he said. 'What is it?'

'Turtle and beans,' I said, deciding not to mention the snails.

'Turtle's good to eat. Did Dad shoot it?'

'If he had,' I said, 'you'd have heard the shot. I caught it by the creek.'

'Well, how about that?'

When he woke my father had Tim hang the birds from a tree branch to keep ants and small animals away from them. 'We'll have a partridge breakfast,' he said. 'And then we'll make an early start.'

We were eating beans from our tin plates. They were slightly underdone but good nevertheless. The turtle tasted just like any other meat, and if I bit into any of the snails, I did not allow myself to think of it.

'Are you well enough to travel?' I asked, worried.

'Both of you listen to me,' said my father. 'A broken leg's not something you can fix in the woods. We've got to find a road. Our best bet is still to float downstream, but this time we've got to watch out for rapids. We'll cut long poles for both of you. When you are in the woods, you can only afford to make one mistake, and we've already made ours. Now we're at the mercy of the weather. And we won't be able to find food. We must get out as soon as humanly possible.'

'I looked for the map,' I said, 'but couldn't find it.'

'It was in my pack,' my father said. 'Don't worry, we won't get lost. We've got to keep our heads and think out each step before we take it. We'll be all right. Both of you are good in the woods, and that's a blessing now. We must avoid being separated, but in case that should happen, remember, just keep going downstream. Sooner or later this creek will run into the Cold River, and I know several trapper's camps there and at least two trails cutting the river.'

'How will you be able to paddle?' I said.

'We'll improvise a back rest,' he said. 'I'll stretch my legs out and manage all right.'

Then as we sat near the comforting fire, he began to talk, slowly and without interruption. At the time I didn't know what he was doing. I realize now that he was giving us his whole life's experience in the woods, with the emphasis on how he caught certain animals or birds, or what he ate in the dead of winter when he had been snowed in on Gore Mountain. Tim found the stories entertaining and forgot them as quickly as he heard them, in his eagerness to hear the next one. I was entertained, too, for it had not seemed to me that my father was old enough to have lived such a varied life. He told us of tricks the Indians had for catching wild geese and turkeys. He described sources of food which I found revolting. 'Grubs and worms are good,' he said. 'You find them under a fallen tree. They're heavy with fat, and that's what you need in the winter. Don't waste an ounce of fat. If you're cooking meat, don't let the fat melt or burn away. It will save your life. Many a man has died for the lack of an ounce of fat.'

The night grew cold, and we huddled together under the two blankets. 'Don't let the fire go out,' warned my father. 'We've got to save our matches.'

'I'll watch it, Dad,' Tim said.

'Let the wild animals hunt for you,' my father said, continuing his dialogue. 'An owl that has caught a rabbit can easily be frightened away from his catch. Even a wolf will run from a man, and you can steal his kill. Though there aren't many wolves in this area any more.'

'What about bears?' Tim asked.

'You can take their kill too,' said my father. 'But only if that's your last chance, because it's dangerous. Be sure you have at least two ways to get away. A tree to climb is good, because even if he tries to follow you up, you can fend him away with a stick. If he has a large kill, such as a deer, you can build a small fire near it and it will keep him away during the night. But always look the country over carefully first, because bears will eat and then sleep nearby.'

'I should think it would be smarter to try and get Mr Bear himself,' I said.

My father laughed. 'You are so right, Miss Lizzy! If you've got a gun, or can trap him, that's just the trick, because the bear has plenty of fat, and as we said, that's just what you need.'

'I saw lots of rabbits,' said Tim. 'They won't come close enough for me to hit them with the paddle, like I did the partridge. But I bet I could get them with a bow and arrow.'

'Yes, you could,' my father agreed. 'But you can fill yourself three times a day with rabbit, or any other white meat, and still starve to death.'

'Oh, Dad,' said Tim. 'Are you kidding me?'

'No, Tim,' my father said seriously. 'Haven't you ever heard of "rabbit starvation"? This disease was well known in the far north. A man can eat his fill of white meat and all he'll get for his trouble is a sick stomach and roaring diarrhœa. In fact, the more he eats, the more hungry he'll become. The only way to get his system back to normal is by adding fat to his diet. Otherwise, he'll die in just a few days. It's actually better to get by on plain water than to eat nothing but rabbit. Of course, if you have good fat grubs, or even dragon-flies, beetles – anything with fat in them – then the rabbit will be all right. Except you must always be sure that it isn't diseased, since many have liver flukes. And you should be careful in cleaning them, since some carry a disease called tularemia. The germs are killed by cooking, so if you are careful to

64

avoid touching the raw meat with any part of your hands that are cut or skinned, you'll be safe enough.'

'I would think that it is hard to starve to death in the woods,' I said.

My father fixed my eyes with his. 'Truer words were never spoken,' he said. 'You'll find game, fish, wild vegetation, insects. Although I wouldn't order them for dessert, you can even eat the common moth. If a bear can stay healthy on grubs and ants, so can you, although I confess that the last time I tried ants, I didn't like them. They were really bitter.'

He laughed, and so did we, and so we drowsed off to sleep, never suspecting what was really in the back of his mind as he entertained us with his delightful tales. Oh, my brave father, alone with your fear and pain, keeping it from us while driving your poor body in a final effort to help us survive! The years between have not dimmed my memory of that night in front of the camp-fire, one of the last happy ones we were ever to have together.

We didn't head down river the next morning nor did we have a partridge breakfast. I'm not sure how my father could have known that he had something more seriously wrong with him than a broken leg, but when we woke up, his face was flushed and he was burning up with fever. When he breathed, it was easy to see that he was in considerable pain. His every breath rasped in his throat. He tried to persuade us to pack up camp and help him to the canoe, but we refused.

'You've caught a bad cold,' I said. 'We're in no danger here on this shore, so it would be foolish to set off today with you sweating with a fever. If we took another spill, the shock of the cold water might stop your heart.'

Reluctantly, he agreed. He was so weak that the mere effort of sitting up to take a few swallows of water turned his face grey and beaded his forehead with sweat. We covered him well and, assuring him we were only going a few hundred yards from camp to hunt for food, went out into the woods.

Tim caught my arm as soon as we were out of earshot. 'Lizzy, what's wrong?' he asked.

'I'm not sure,' I said, 'but I think he has pneumonia.'

Tim said, 'How can that be? It's only been a day since he got wet.'

'He may have been carrying the germs for some time, and it only took the dunking to set them off. His leg isn't infected, so the fever can't be caused by that.'

'Maybe it's just flu,' Tim said.

'I hope so.'

'What do we do?'

'We must keep him quiet and warm, unless the fever goes too high, in which case we'll have to bring it down with cold compresses.'

Tim stared at me. 'You're a whiz-bang wonder,' he said. 'How do you know all these things?'

'I heard Miss Pauline describing how her mother was treated for pneumonia,' I said.

'And that made her well?'

'No,' I said, hesitating. 'She died anyway.'

My father's spirits had risen when we returned an hour later with a handsome catch. I had picked spruce needles to boil down for tea, and while I was occupied, Tim came upon a porcupine, unfrightened behind its fortress of quills. He killed it with a stick and gingerly brought it back to camp, where my father was sipping some of the refreshing spruce tea.

'This lazybones will give us plenty of fat,' Tim said. 'I'll toss it in the fire and burn off the quills to make him easy to clean.'

'No,' my father said in a low voice. 'That won't work. You'll have to skin him out very carefully. Make your incision along the belly and be sure you don't get a quill in your hand. It can fester.'

Tim took almost an hour to skin the porcupine. It was hard going, but later that night we agreed it was worth the effort, because the roasted meat and especially the liver, which was large enough to serve each of us a generous portion, was as delicious as pork. My father ate heartily, and this gladdened me. I started to come around to Tim's suggestion of the flu.

Again, as we lay under the stars, warming ourselves at the cheerful fire, my father told us more stories of his adventures in the woods. Yet for all my new hope, I couldn't help but notice that he seemed to be addressing his words more to me than to Tim. Yet Tim was our woodsman. I had never had any real talents for the outdoor life. I might remember what my father said, but it would take Tim to carry out his suggestions. I could never in a million years have skinned our supper. Tim was clumsy and slow, but with proper guidance, he had got the job done.

'You would be surprised at the half-baked things I have seen men lost in the woods do,' my father was saying. 'Why, would you believe that one man out of three, one who has been lost for days and who comes out on to a wilderness road, a strange road, one that is not the one he is looking for, will actually turn back into the woods and get himself *more* lost because he has found the wrong road? That is silly – and don't forget it.' He stared at me. 'You won't forget it, will you, Miss Lizzy?'

'No Father,' I said. 'I will try to remember.'

'Good,' he said, coughing again. The rasping in his throat was rougher than it had been in the evening. I got up and poured him the last of the spruce tea, serving it in the one tin cup that had survived our capsizing. He thanked me and sipped at it, thinking all the while.

'I am depending on you,' he said, looking at me. 'Your brother is a good woodsman, but there is too much for him to learn so fast. You must remember what I say and remind him.'

My heart sank. He seemed to be telling me goodbye. I said quickly, 'Yes, and we will both do what you tell us. If your fever is better, we'll be on our way in the morning, and in two days we will find a road and no matter what road it is, Tim will walk out for help while I stay with you.'

He didn't answer, because another coughing fit took

him and when it was over he lay back, weak and pale.

During the night, as I feared, his fever did rise until it burned my hand to press it against his forehead. He was sweating, and tried to throw off the blankets, but I was wary of the chill air and of cooling him too rapidly. We applied wet rags to his head and neck, which seemed to soothe him. He spoke, often, to my mother, dead so long ago, and I had to give Tim a hard kick in the ribs because he had started to cry and I didn't want my father to hear him.

Dawn came none too soon for me, for it seemed as if the night had gone on for years. We had one of the remaining partridges, and I brewed some more spruce tea, which we tried to get my father to eat. But he was not interested in food, though he sipped some of the tea. He didn't speak. I saw there was no hope of our trying to go downstream today, either. His eyes were listless and dull, and once I saw a tear there, too, and it almost dissolved me into a spell of weeping myself. But I sternly reminded myself that I could not show fear or uncertainty to my father, for he needed all the confidence he could muster.

Tim hunted all day and came back with two more birds and some eggs he had robbed from a nest. We scrambled the eggs and fried them in a bit of porcupine fat, and my father was able to choke down a few mouthfuls. As evening came on, Tim said thoughtlessly: 'Are you going to tell us some stories tonight, Dad?' My father tried, but it was painful for him to speak. He had been coughing up white sputum flecked with rusty spots, and had a rag pressed against his mouth most of the time.

'Tonight is my turn to be the storyteller,' I said. 'Father, what would you like to hear?'

He made a weak gesture that could have meant anything, and I plunged recklessly into the first thing that came to mind. It happened to be one that I had read during the summer when we had visited our cousins in Bolton Landing, and I had chanced on a book of stories by Mark Twain.

I recited the opening chapters of *Tom Sawyer* for almost an hour, until my father and Tim were both asleep. Then I turned on my side and cried.

In the morning, my father was cold and still. We would not believe that he was gone, but nothing we could do would bring him back. Tim went a little crazy and ran yelling into the woods. It was only when I had covered my father with the blankets that I could coax Tim back. It took us most of the day to hack out a shallow grave, using the axe and canoe paddle. Then I had to strike Tim in the face to force him to help me roll my father into it. We covered him softly with the fresh earth, both of us crying, for I had decided that we must take both blankets and so there was nothing to keep the dirt out of his unprotected eyes. Tim was useless at the grave, so I finished there while he piled the gear carelessly into the canoe. We shoved father's revolver down to the bottom of the pack and just as the sun touched the treetops pushed off downstream. There were words that I remembered from the Bible. I suppose I could have said them over my father, but I was so angry over the senselessness and injustice of what had happened that I wanted to curse God instead. I did not, because, secretly, I guess, I was afraid of what He might do in return.

TWO

The Cabin

The next morning I began to work carefully on my calendar. It became the most precious of my few personal possessions. It was a thick sheet of birch bark which I carried packed inside the large pot. I wrote on it with a stick of charred wood I had taken from one of our campfires. It was only one day since we had buried my father in a shallow grave and fled downstream like two thieves pursued by Justice. Why we did not capsize a second time and die in those cold, rushing waters that awful afternoon is beyond me to answer. Tim tried to keep the canoe under control, but he didn't have the skill or the attention that day to do more than provide enough steerageway to keep us from whirling around like a runaway log. We slid wildly from one shore to the other, with me fending off threatening rocks and logs with a long pole. It was as if we were in guilty flight, as if we were somehow responsible for what had happened in that lonely clearing in the woods. We had to put it behind us, for neither of us had the courage to spend another night there.

But daylight soon deserted us, and we were forced to come ashore some three or four miles downstream. Tim pulled the canoe up on a sandy beach and began unloading it as I stacked stones for a campfire. My hands were trembling, and it took me three precious matches to get the blaze going. By then it was almost dark. Tim and I huddled next to the fire, wrapped in the blankets, shivering more from fear than from cold, no browse bed made and no stories to tell in the darkness. I don't believe either of us slept, nor did we talk. Each crept into the little shell we save for such hours of despair and loneliness and stayed the night there, alone and forlorn.

When morning came, the canoe was gone; it had drifted away during the night. There must have been rain far upstream somewhere, causing the creek to rise slightly, just enough to slip the unsecured canoe off the beach and take it downstream without a sound. We searched for it half the day and finally gave up.

Angered, I shouted at Tim: 'You should have been more careful!'

He hung his head. 'I know.'

But I was foolish and did not let up. 'How could you have been so dumb? It's your fault.'

'Not everything is my fault!' he flared. 'Whose idea was it to come down this terrible Cold River? Dad was willing to go back. If you had let him, he might be alive now.'

I sat down, sick to my stomach.

He saw the anguish on my face and softened. He touched my shoulder. 'I'm sorry, Lizzy,' he said. 'I didn't mean that.'

'You are right. My wilfulness killed my father.'

'It was only an accident,' he said. 'A canoe can overturn anywhere.'

'Leave me alone,' I said.

He looked away. I think he was crying.

Well, there was no future in sitting on the bank of a river feeling sorry for ourselves.

'We will have to make a raft,' I said. 'If we cut dry logs we can –'

I stopped. The expression on Tim's face was ghastly.

'I left the axe in the canoe,' he said.

I had no words for him. His carelessness in beaching the canoe had cost us its use. His failure to take the axe out of it had perhaps cost us our lives.

'I've still got my knife.'

'We can't cut logs for a raft with a pocket knife,' I said.

'What are we going to do?' he asked.

'I don't know,' I said. 'Let me think. You go and see if you can find something for us to eat. I'll soak some

71

beans meanwhile. We had better plan on staying here tonight.'

He left, glad for something to do. I sat down and stared at the water rushing past.

There was no way now for us to follow this branch of Cold River. We'd be lucky to do three or four miles a day along its banks. The walking, without a trail, would be too difficult.

No, we would have to set off cross-country. I hoped Tim still had his compass. I tried to remember the lay of the land. I knew that there were hundreds of square miles of wilderness around us. But it seemed to me that by striking off southeast, we would stand the best chance of cutting a trail or coming on some sign of human habitation.

I got the fire going again and put a handful of beans in the pot to soak. Now that we would be walking, it would not be possible for us to carry all the gear. We would have to take only that which would be the most useful.

We needed at least one of the pots, that was sure. And the matches and the blankets. There were just a couple of pounds of beans left, and some salt. The extra clothes could be worn, unless the days got too warm.

As I wrestled with plans for the next day, I took off my boots and with my feet felt around in the clean sand where the canoe had been. I soon found half a dozen clams, and after rinsing them off, I put them in the pot. When the water was warm, they opened up. I pried them out and threw the shells away, and put their meat back in the pot. The beans were soaking in the other pot. It would be an hour or more until they were ready to put on the fire.

There being nothing left to do, I sat down and, with a strip of birch bark and an ember from the fire, made the first notation on what was to become my calendar.

Tim came back empty-handed and shamefaced. 'I'm sorry, Lizzy,' he said. 'I saw one partridge, but it got away.'

'That's all right,' I said. 'We have some clams and the

beans. We won't starve. But we have to make the best use of our time. Do you still have your compass?'

'Yes,' he said, happy to be of some help. He gave it to me. I held it up. The needle didn't move.

'You've got water in it,' I said. I shook it. Sluggishly the needle began to swing. I checked it against the sun. Yes, if you were willing to wait, the instrument would point to the north.

'What have you decided?' Tim asked.

This made me mad. 'I have decided,' I said, 'that you are the leader of this expedition and that you should stop looking to me for every little suggestion.'

He gave a confused wave of his hand. 'But you're older,' he said.

'And you've been in the woods twice as much as I have. You take the lead. I'll follow. When I think of something that will help, I'll tell you.'

I had spent some time while I searched for the clams working out this approach. Tim was frightened and erratic just now, because my father's death had scoured him of his natural toughness, but when it came back, he would be much more effective in planning the bold strokes that were necessary to rescue us from our forest predicament. I would back him up and recite as much of what my father had told us as seemed necessary. I saw immediately that my decision was the right one.

'All right,' Tim said. 'We're going to have to walk out.'

I already knew that, but I said nothing. 'Which way?' I asked.

'Well . . . the creek's running northeast.'

'Won't it be hard following its banks, though?'

'Yes, I guess it would. Maybe we'd better head due east.' He paused and then said, 'No, southeast. That ought to get us to a town quicker than any other direction. But we'll have to walk around a couple of mountains, if I remember that map right.'

'We can take our time,' I said. 'We'll hunt and gather food as we go, so that we will always have something to eat.'

73

'But we can't fool around too long,' he said. 'You have to remember, we can get snow up here the first of November.'

I put the beans on to boil. 'A little snow won't hurt us,' I said. 'But we must be very careful not to overtire ourselves to the point where we become careless again.'

'I know,' he said. Then: 'Lizzy, I'm sorry.'

'It wasn't really your fault. The creek rose overnight.'

'I meant about your father.'

'Oh.'

I wanted to say, *But he was your father too*, but couldn't.

While I fed the fire he took his knife and cut some spruce branches for our bed and had it all ready by the time the food was ready to eat. We sat near the fire after the meal and watched the sky darken.

Tim touched my shoulder. 'Don't you worry, Lizzy, I'll get you home safe.'

I would have laughed, what with the blind leading the blind, except that my eyes were flooded with tears and I had to gulp down a huge lump in my throat before I could choke, 'I know, Timmy.'

Next morning, we ate the cold beans that remained from the previous evening's meal. We divided our gear. Tim made two makeshift packs from the blankets, and we stowed the gear in them, with the two pots tied on behinds like soldiers' helmets. I was glad to have the second pot.

We took a careful reading with the compass, checked it against the rising sun, and were on our way before the morning birds had finished their serenade to the dawn. As we came upon fallen trees, we broke off limbs to use for walking sticks and to throw at game, and each time we found a better stick we threw away the old one, until finally we were both armed with stout, heavy cudgels. We paused often to consult the compass, and made it a point always to line up two objects in the distance before setting off again. It might be a tree and a distant knoll, but whatever our marks, we did not allow ourselves to

74

be seduced into taking the easy way around, which would have lost us our landmarks.

The hills were steep, and we lost time in climbing up them. But we didn't try to thread our way between them, which would soon have led us in a circle. We kept our eyes open for game but saw none. When we paused late in the afternoon, as the sun touched the trees, we did so because we had come upon water, which we hadn't seen for several hours.

'We'd better stay here,' Tim said. 'At least we'll have water.'

'You start the fire,' I said. 'I think I can find us some greens.'

I had seen some pigweed a few hundred yards back and soon found it again. I didn't want to exhaust our supply of beans any sooner than was necessary. I remembered that the entire plant was edible, including its stalks and longish pale green leaves. I gathered a large bundle in minutes and on my way back to camp was delighted to come on a young spruce tree which provided fresh needles for tea.

The pigweed greens boiled down to where they furnished only a bare meal for the two of us. I made a mental note to gather twice as many next time. But the spruce tea was warm and filling.

Since the moss under the trees was soft, we did without a browse bed that night and were comfortable enough, although we both fell into a deep sleep and the fire burned out before dawn.

In the morning we had some hot spruce tea and were on our way. We picked some berries which were small and bitter, but we ate them anyway as we walked.

This day was luckier. Tim motioned me with his hand to a stop. Then, before I saw what he was swinging at, he caught a sitting rabbit a crashing blow with his stick. He gutted it out and tied it to his belt. An hour later, we came on a big grey grouse nesting in a tree. It flew away, but I climbed up and stole the eggs and put them in my pocket. About sunset, we found water, a small stream which ran towards the east and west, and made camp there. There were nettles along the shore. I had read somewhere that they made tender eating when boiled, so I picked some and tried them in a pot with a little water and the eggs, which were somewhat ripe. The result was not the most delicious soup we ever had, but it seemed to satisfy the hunger in me, which, I think, must have been the beginning of a desire for fat.

Tim cut the rabbit into four pieces which we roasted over the coals and ate them later, after dark. They were so good that I found it hard to believe that such a diet could be harmful in the long run.

If things had proceeded as they did these first two days, I think we would have walked out that first week. But luck did not stay with us.

We were crossing a ravine on a large fallen tree, which was the only way to get to the other side without crawling down a rocky ledge. Tim went over easily enough, but as I followed, my feet suddenly shot from under me, and for a terrible moment I thought I was going to crash all the way to the bottom. I was lucky enough to come down on the log again, although with a terrific crash. I clung there until Tim crawled out and helped me over. What had happened was that the wood was rotten, and I had put my foot in such a way that the bark simply sloughed off, leaving bare peeled wood and me, dangling in mid-air.

When I tried to stand, a terrible pain shot up my leg. For a moment I was sure I had broken it, just as my father had. But as it began to swell, I recognized the injury as a sprain, something that was no stranger to energetic youngsters who lived near the woods.

I tried to hobble on it, but the pain was too much for me; I had to sit down every ten feet or so. Tim decided that I was not fit to go on, so he made me comfortable and began looking around for a place to make a camp. He listened carefully, thought he heard the sound of water, and then followed his ears. He was right. There was a small spring, tumbling from beneath a huge boulder. Tim came back and helped me get there slowly, then returned for my pack.

We were to spend ten days in that spot. Before we were able to leave, the first snow had filtered down through the tall trees.

Making a proper camp was more difficult because of not having an axe, but we managed. We did not, of course, realize that we would be stuck here for over a week, or we would have constructed a larger lean-to. Instead, since I was barely able to hobble around, we made a rude shelter by placing three long branches up against a tall rock and then covering them with boughs. Tim brought more boughs for a browse bed underneath and, in just a couple of hours, we were protected from the elements, although a bit crowded. We placed the campfire just outside the entrance to the shelter. While the daylight lasted, Tim gathered firewood, which again was made more difficult by not having an axe to cut it into convenient lengths. Still, he did well. While he worked, I boiled some beans. As they were cooking, I turned over some stones and found a variety of white grubs and two small beetles. I decided to release the beetles, but I dropped the grubs into the pot with the beans, averting my eyes as I did so and resolving not to mention them to Tim. Luckily, they cooked down and mixed with the beans so as not to be noticeable. I looked about for edible greens but didn't see any near enough to identify.

Tim had searched for game or eggs but didn't find either. He did bring me some spruce needles for tea, however, which I put on to boil while we ate.

He smacked his lips over the beans. 'These are good.' I thought of the white grubs and bit my lip. Perhaps it would have done no harm to tell him, but why take the chance? As for me, now that the awful deed had been done, I had no regrets and gave the matter little thought. Food was life, and this was no time to be squeamish. In later years, when I travelled and came upon my first raw oyster, I saw the amusement in the eyes of my companions and their surprise when I gulped the shellfish down without flinching. When you have eaten white grubs from under a rock, there is no oyster in the world that can scare you.

I think we would have been out of that camp in a day or two if I had not over-exerted myself the next morning, trying to do too much. My ankle swelled up to twice its normal size and turned an angry red. But I was determined to preserve our meagre supply of beans. As soon as Tim had gone off hunting, I set out to look for food. I made him promise not to go more than half a mile from camp and to blaze an occasional tree with his knife. We were so deep in the woods that it would be all too easy to wander in circles. While we were together, we had a chance of getting out alive; alone we would have no chance at all.

I found some wild grapevines, and, although the birds had been at them, there were still a few small bunches of grapes. I took all I found. While they weren't plump, but rather dried up like raisins, I was glad to have them.

On the way back to camp, I came across a patch of slim, narrow-leaved plants in a clearing. I broke off one tip of a leaf and tasted it. There was a pronounced flavour of onion. I dug down a few inches in the ground. Sure enough, I unearthed many white bulbs which I recognized as wild onions. I took enough for a hearty meal and made a mental note of the spot. The onions would be healthy and would give us needed vitamins that might be missing in our diet of meat and beans, assuming that Tim came back with some meat.

To my delight, he did. It was an almost full-grown partridge. With that and the onions, we wouldn't have to dig into our beans.

He was very excited. 'I saw some wild turkeys,' he said. 'Big as a house. If only I'd thought to take the pistol – '

'No, Tim,' I said. 'You would only waste the ammunition and perhaps shoot yourself in the foot. How far away were they?'

'Just down the hill,' he said. 'They flew up in the trees

when they saw me.'

'Perhaps we can trap them,' I said.

'With a snare? We've got the fishing-line.'

'Don't you remember the Indian trick my father told us about?' He didn't, so I repeated it. Then he nodded.

'Do you think that would really work?'

'We will only have to risk a few beans to find out. I think a wild turkey might be partial to pinto beans when there's no corn to be had.'

'Okay,' he said. 'I'll cut some sticks.'

While he did so, I scalded the partridge in the pot of water I had been heating over the fire and then plucked it clean. I had to wait until he had finished with the knife to take off the head and open up the cavity to remove the innards. I saved the liver, heart, and gizzard and wrapped the rest in a leaf. Perhaps the guts would come in handy as a lure for a wild animal.

We cut the partridge into small pieces and put it into the pot to boil, along with some salt and the wild onions. I covered the pot and put it far enough from the fire so there was no chance of its boiling over or burning. We would have a nice supper waiting when we returned. It would be welcome, for our only breakfast had been the leftover beans from the night before.

As Tim helped me hobble down the hill towards where he had seen the turkeys, I noticed several small runways among the trees where various animals had been going back and forth. 'We must set some snares and deadfalls along here,' I said, pointing them out to him. 'They can work for us while we sleep.'

He left me behind a log and crept down the slope to the spot where the turkeys had been feeding on acorns. I watched as he constructed the trap my father had described. Very simple, it was based on the assumption that a wild turkey is not much smarter than a chunk of wood. I accepted this view, since I have heard of turkeys that stood out in the rain with their heads tilted up until they drowned because they were too stupid to lower their backs.

Tim built a small four-sided pen with four posts and

branches tied between them, making a square with the branches about a foot off the ground. Then he baited the trap with a few precious beans and slipped back up the hill to hide with me behind the log. We waited, speaking only in whispers.

'Do you have your club?' I asked.

He showed it to me, a heavy branch as long as his arm, with an evil-looking knot at one end. 'If they behave like you say,' he told me, 'I'll let them have it with this.'

We waited for most of the day, not daring to move. Several times I almost gave up. Perhaps the turkeys had been frightened away for good. Perhaps they had never existed except in Tim's imagination.

The sun moved across the sky and the pain in my leg intensified. I was ready to call it a day when there came a flapping sound. Out of the corner of my eye, I saw a large, dark shape land ungracefully near our trap. Tim gave a start, and I quieted him with a whispered 'shhh.'

The turkey examined the beans as if they were strange relations come to call unexpectedly. Now was the important part. If he stood up and stretched his neck over the bar to eat the beans, all was lost.

But, as my father had predicted, the lazy turkey took the easy way. He put his neck *under* the bar and began to gobble up the bait. Tim stirred at my side.

'Wait,' I said. 'If he's not caught, you'll just scare him away. If the trap doesn't work and we don't frighten him, maybe we can catch him some other way tomorrow.'

There was no need to fear. My father was right, as always. Mr Tom Turkey – fat, dumb, and stupid – completed his meal, lifted his head, and felt the bar press against the back of his neck. He gave a squawking gobble and shook his body. But so far as he knew, he had been seized by some terrifying enemy, and being only an ignorant turkey, gave his soul up to the Almighty.

That wild turkey was too dense to lower his head under the single bar of the foot-high fence Tim had built!

'Get him,' I told Tim who rushed down the hill, brandishing his club. He was upon the turkey before the frightened bird knew what was in the wind. As Tim took a mighty swing, I hoped his aim was good. It was. He struck the big bird square across the back, and there was a solid cracking sound as the bones broke. The fence broke, too, and the turkey got loose, but Tim didn't give it a chance to escape. He hit it again with the club and then threw himself on to it and caught it by the neck with one hand, fumbling his knife out with the other. The turkey threw itself about in a cloud of leaves and moss. Once I was sure Tim had lost it, but when he brought his knife into play and cut off the bird's head, leaping back as the blood spurted and the huge yellow feet thrashed on the forest floor.

'Tie the neck!' I yelled. 'Save the blood!'

Tim took a piece of fishing line from his pocket and knotted it around the bird's neck. The turkey had stopped struggling. Tim stood up, gasping. There was fresh blood on his hands and arms.

He hefted the bird. 'It's so heavy I can hardly pick it up!'

'I'll help you.' But when I stood the pain in my ankle was so bad that it was all I could do to keep from crying out in pain. Tim saw my distress and shouted, 'You stay there. I can make it.'

And he did, puffing and gasping for breath, half-dragging the limp carcass of the turkey.

Worried, he asked: 'Are you all right?'

'It's only my ankle,' I said. 'Take the turkey to camp. I'll follow.'

Burdened as he was, he still soon out-distanced me. I wasn't halfway back to camp when he reappeared empty-handed to help me. His aid was welcome, and as I lowered myself on to the blanket-covered browse bed, it was with a sigh of welcome relief.

But there was work to be done before our catch cooled. 'Tie our Tom up by his feet,' I said, 'and put the extra pot under his neck to collect all the blood.'

'Why?'

'It's the richest part of the food,' I said. 'Four table-spoons of blood are as nutritious as ten large hen's eggs.'

Repulsed, he said. 'But we can't drink blood.'

'I'll use it in soup,' I said. 'Hurry, before it gets clotted.'

He did as I had suggested. Soon there was the steady dripping of the bird's blood into the pot. Meanwhile, I built up the fire and put our supper closer to it, for the partridge was not quite done; I had left it too far from the coals.

I estimated that the wild turkey would dress out to perhaps fifteen or sixteen pounds. He looked fat and sassy, too, and I hoped that there were the ingredients for two or three pots of rich turkey soup under his ribs, in addition to the hearty white and dark meat he would provide.

'Tim, I'm proud of you. We'll eat well for a week, thanks to today's work.'

'It was you who remembered how to catch him,' he said loyally.

'Wash the blood off your hands and lie down to rest,' I said. 'I'll wake you when supper is ready.'

Tim dozed for perhaps an hour. When he woke, I served up the partridge stew, which was delicious. He asked me where I had found the onions. When I told him, he promised to dig some more. 'I'm going to take the guts of the partridge and use them to bait a deadfall,' he said. 'Maybe I can catch a coon or a fox.'

'Please do not catch a bear,' I said. 'I don't think I'm up to cleaning one today.'

He laughed. It was a good sound to hear. He took some extra twine and went down the hill while I tidied up after the meal. The turkey had almost bled itself out. Since it was too big to scald, I cut it down and began to pluck the feathers. I saved the bigger ones, which might be useful later, tied to a fish hook. The rest I put in a careful pile. I could not think of any purpose for them, but there was no point in throwing away anything which might be of future use.

The blood, which had half filled the pot, I put aside

after adding about a third of it to our leftover partridge stew. I intended to use the remainder for a pot of soup from the turkey fat and giblets.

Since Tim had the knife, I could not open up the bird, but I did get all the smallest pinfeathers off. We could singe the rest over the fire, but it would take the two of us to hold the heavy turkey.

Tim returned, and we attended to that task, he holding the bird by the feet and I by the neck. We revolved it slowly over the low fire and smelled the pungent singeing of the remaining feathers. It reminded me of home and was almost enough to make me cry. Instead, I berrated Tim for letting one wing sink down into the coals. 'Don't burn the fat away,' I complained. 'You're too careless.'

He started to give me a quick answer, but swallowed it. 'I set the deadfall,' he said. 'Now I'll get some more onions.'

'Bring the tops too,' I said. 'We can cook them down in the soup.'

He left the knife which I used to clean out the turkey — not as difficult as I had feared. I saved the liver, which was very large, and the heart and the gizzard, as I had done that morning with the partridge. I diced half of the liver and put it in the partridge soup to begin cooking. I put the rest and the heart, cut into four pieces, into the other pot with the rest of the turkey blood. I filled it almost to the top with water and put it by the fire to simmer. I skewered the gizzard on a stick and broiled it carefully over the fire so that it was deliciously golden brown when Tim returned with his harvest. He protested when I gave him the whole gizzard, and I said: 'You know perfectly well that I'm not fond of gizzards,' so he ate it all.

Meanwhile I cut all of the visible fat away from the inside of the turkey's cavity and added the best part of it to the larger pot which contained the innards and most of the blood. I put one or two chunks into the other pot to sweeten the partridge stew. Tim finished eating the gizzard and wiped his mouth on the back of his hand. 'I was hungry again,' he said. 'But we only finished eating an hour ago.'

'It was probably the lack of fat that made you hungry so soon,' I said. 'But our friend, Tom Turkey, will fill that bill.'

According to my instructions, Tim hung the carcass up again to keep it away from crawling insects. I wished we had a muslin cloth to protect it from flies, but there weren't many flies in the woods that late in the season.

It was growing dark now. Tim spent half an hour gathering more firewood which he had to break with his foot. I could see that he sorely missed the axe but he didn't mention it.

When night was fully upon us, we sat at the edge of the shelter, toasting our feet in front of the fire. 'It's colder today – did you notice?' Tim asked.

'Yes. But the cold shouldn't bother us if we're prudent. It will help us preserve fresh food such as your friend the turkey.'

Tim laughed. 'I didn't think any bird could be so silly.'

'There are many things in the woods that are hard to believe,' I said.

'Well, we'd be in real trouble without the things you know.'

'I don't know anything,' I said gently. 'It was my father who knew these things. It's he who will save us.'

My ankle was too sore for me to move the following day, so I spent most of the time cutting up the turkey and partially cooking the pieces, hoping that cooked meat would keep longer than raw. The fire had burned down to a single ember when we awoke. We spent some time blowing on it, against twists of birch bark, to build it up again without wasting a match. But soon it was burning nicely and dispelling the chill in the morning air.

'Do you think you'll be able to walk any time soon?' Tim asked, worried. I shook my head. 'Then I'll gather some more stones and wood today and build a reflector for this fire to throw its heat up inside the shelter. This way, most of the heat is going straight up in the air.'

I thought that was a sensible idea and said so. He set off to check his deadfall while I heated up the partridge stew. He came back glum-faced. Something had sneaked around the deadfall and stolen his bait, but was not trapped.

'We have more bait,' I said. 'Don't be discouraged. How did you make the deadfall, anyway?'

'I used a heavy log. I propped it up with a stick and tied some of the partridge guts to the stick. The rest I scattered around to draw the animal in.'

'Did you put it right on the runway?'

'Yes.'

'Then you did everything right. Of course, when you set it again, you might narrow the runway with some more logs, so that the only way the animal can get to the bait is to walk directly under the deadfall, instead of approaching from the side or the rear, which is what must have happened.'

I could see him digesting this new thought, gradually understanding and accepting it. 'Yes,' he said finally, 'I think that would help.'

'Eat your stew,' I said. 'It's hot, and the turkey fat has added a nice flavour.' I gave him a hearty portion. Then I said: 'The only other thing I remember about deadfalls is something Indian Pete once told me, about putting the prop stick on a small pebble. That makes it even easier to dislodge when the animal touches the stick.'

Tim chewed on a piece of partridge and nodded. 'I'll fix it that way,' he said. 'And I'm going to set some rabbit snares, too. I found two runways that are so fresh they were almost warm.' He looked at the turkey, which was still hanging. (It was only later in the day that I cut it up.) 'But we don't want to get so much meat that it spoils before we can eat it.'

I laughed. 'Don't worry about that, dear Tim. You bring me all the meat you can carry. I'll see to the rest.'

He took the turkey innards and, after cutting some lengths of twine, left me his knife and went off to rebait the deadfall and set his snares.

He and I had set snares before for rabbits and had even caught some, for in those days the rabbits lived very close to the farm. I understand that they run in seven-year cycles. The year before we went on our ill-fated canoe trip, they had been on the increase. It seemed as if they were everywhere, bounding down the old logging roads at your approach, their fluffy white tails following like a stuck-on powderpuff. A rabbit snare is not difficult to make. The simplest is made by suspending a loop of heavy twine across a well-used runway, tied securely to a branch overhead and fastened lightly to a small stake driven into the ground. The rabbit, in its usual hurry to be about its business, comes bounding down its customary trail and runs its neck through the loop, the knot slips, and it strangles himself in its efforts to get away. A fancier method is to suspend the loops from a bent-over branch which is held under tension by a small knot fastened through another stake driven in the ground. When the rabbit plunges into the loop, it pulls the knot loose from the stake, and the bent branch snaps up. This not only hastens the rabbit's end, because it will not have any support for its powerful rear legs, but keeps it above the depradations of marauding foxes and dogs which might have evil designs on your catch. Tim was an expert at both kinds of snares. I knew he would do a good job. Even with my father's warnings about 'rabbit starvation' well in mind, it would still be pleasant to have an abundance of meat even if some of it was only fit for filling our bellies.

I parboiled the turkey over a heap of coals scraped away from the main fire. One of the difficulties the tenderfoot has in the woods is when he tries to cook over an open flame. Such a fire is cheerful, but you can't cook well over it. You must have glowing coals. They did a beautiful job on our turkey. As each piece was finished, I wrapped it in ferns and piled it on the one small scrap of canvas we had remaining after the canoe had drifted away. When Tim returned, I would have him tie it up in a tree.

I also attended to the second pot of stew. The mixture of blood and water had boiled down halfway, so I added more water, and after tasting it, some salt. You wouldn't have known the stew's ingredients if you hadn't seen me put them in. The wild onions and their green tops made a splendid addition.

I put one turkey drumstick aside, for it would be nice to have some solid food to eat with our stew, and covered the rest with the canvas.

Since Tim was nowhere in sight, I crawled over to the far side of the fire and, with a stone, began pounding branches into the ground to form a support for a reflector. I was nearly finished when he came up the hill. We had the job done in a matter of minutes, using three small logs piled against the branches to gather the heat and throw it towards the opening of our rude shelter.

Tim was hungry, so I gave him the wild grapes I had picked the day before and which had lain, wrapped in a cloth, forgotten. He said they were bitter, but he ate them all.

The swelling of my ankle was still very pronounced. I remembered the last time I had a bad sprain, that it was the better part of a week before I could hobble about. There was no point in setting off again so soon that I would not be able to keep up with the pace, so I told Tim bluntly that it would be at least a week before we could move.

'Maybe I ought to go ahead and get help,' he suggested.

'I thought of that. But are you sure you could find your way back here?'

'No,' he said slowly. 'Even if I blazed trees, I could still miss them coming in.'

'You do as you think best,' I said. 'Either way, we are taking a gamble. If we stay, we are betting that the weather doesn't get too bad for us to travel later. If you go, our bet is that you will be able to find me again.'

'And that I don't get lost along the way or hurt myself, or make some mistake.' He shook his head. 'No, Lizzy, I think it's safer for both of us if I stay with you. We seem to be all right for food, so the weather is all we have to worry about.'

'Very well,' I said. 'Now that we've reached our decision, let's make the best of it. I think you ought to put more boughs on our roof. A bough roof is no place in the rain anyway, but if there's merely a drizzle, maybe we can keep it out.'

'I'll do that,' he said. 'When do we eat?'

'Get me some spruce needles for tea. Then I'll cook us a big turkey drumstick while you fix the roof.'

He got the spruce. When I saw them, I noticed that he had got a few hemlock mixed in with the rest. I remembered that some Greek named Socrates was forced to drink hemlock and died, so I was very concerned and made a strong point with Tim that he should be careful not to mistake the hemlock for spruce. Hemlock needles grow in spirals and are flatter than other pines. We had no troubles on this score from then on, although I was convinced that my vigilance had saved us from instant poisoning. You can imagine my embarrassment when, years later, I learned that the North American hemlock evergreen conifer has no family relationship to the poisonous member of the parsley family which was used for the deadly potions of the Greek ancients.

In 1921 we were not as vitamin-conscious as health-oriented people are today. But we were well aware, from hard observation, of the dangers of badly balanced diet, including the dreaded scurvy which didn't strike just the members of Captain Bligh's ill-fated *Bounty*. Trappers in the far north faced grave risk of this disease, particularly when their food was overcooked and its vitamin C was destroyed. It was because spruce tea – indeed, tea made from any evergreen needles – was especially high in ascorbic acid that scurvy ceased to be a problem with those northern travellers who would take the time and use the common sense to brew up a batch once every day or so.

I broiled the drumstick carefully, dipping it every now and then into the rich stew so that when it was done, it was glazed and fragrant. Tim and I dined handsomely on it and some stew. I took what was left and put it in the stew along with the large bone, which I broke first.

In telling this story, I have noticed that perhaps I have seemed to make too much of food, but then, there's a reason for that. At this stage shelter was no real problem. There was no recreation or diversion other than trying to keep ourselves fed, so our thoughts and actions were constantly oriented towards the capture, preparation, and consumption of food. Food is life, and we were determined to keep our sights fixed constantly on the preservation of our lives.

During my life I have heard numerous friends complain: 'I'm not getting anywhere in life,' or 'Oh, I have lost my job, and whatever will I do now,' or 'I do not see how I can go on much longer, things are so difficult.' It is always my first inclination to laugh at these poor souls. What do they know of life, of raw survival, or not knowing from one day to the next if you will breathe under another sun? What is there to fear? These unlucky people build their own traps. Not getting anywhere in life? Well, where do you want to get? As Bernard Shaw said: 'You must make sure to get what you like, or you will be forced to like what you get.' Many a runner has fallen short of the tape because he did not care – or exert himself – enough to win that victory. What claim has he for complaint? Another better man won, that is all. If you cannot get the first place you would like, then you must like the second place you can get.

As for those who have lost jobs or who see their high standards of living in danger, I say, 'So what?' Who on earth or in heaven or down below ever promised us that we would have things easy all our lives? Is a child born clutching a contract guaranteeing him a colour television set and two cars in the garage? You will notice that all of these complaints deal exclusively with *things*. Few seem to despair that they have not achieved all that it was within them to do, but rather take issue with the size of the rewards they have received. I know that the grass is always greener but I have tried to remain content with the size of my pasture, to rejoice when an unexpected plum falls my way. But this is a hard attitude to preserve when one is surrounded by malcontents whose only real goal in life seems to be sure that they have gotten every scrap of 'what is coming to them' and who would rather not be bothered with the obvious question (to me, at least) of, 'what have you done to deserve it?' Apparently, merely being alive is reason enough, although as you can tell, I quarrel violently with that notion. It is amazing how little one really *needs* and how quickly you can give the rest up when it becomes necessary. Most of us could stand a little refreshment in this truth.

At any rate, food was at the head of our list there in the forest, and Tim and I spent every waking moment taking care of that problem. We had many other difficulties, but it was rare for us to go hungry – nor is there any reason for any levelheaded person to do so; no matter how lost he is.

We never had a problem with food spoiling, since the weather was growing steadily colder. But we might well have faced such difficulty during the summer. It is not boastful to say that I think we ate as well as any camper who was not lost, and perhaps better than some.

Those days we camped there by the spring were, in retrospect, a tempering period, an adjustment to being alone in the wilderness. Perhaps for that reason, it was a good thing I had sprained my ankle: we gained time to take our own measure, to determine what we could and could not do.

On the third morning, for example, Tim came rushing up the hill. A large raccoon was caught in his deadfall, but it was still alive.

'I think I'd better shoot him,' Tim said.

I knew Tim had been aching to shoot my father's pistol, but I had no alternative, for I didn't know if it were possible for Tim to kill the animal with his club. Reluctantly I agreed, and he went off carrying the big .44 Colt carefully.

A few minutes later I heard the shot and immediately

after it, a shout. My heart chilled. Had Tim somehow managed to shoot himself? I called out, then again, and heard an answer.

In a while, Tim came up the hill. He had the pistol, but no raccoon. I asked him what had happened.

Sheepishly he confessed that he had missed and hit the deadfall instead of the raccoon beneath it. Furthermore, he had underestimated the recoil, and the pistol had bucked back, bruising his thumb. In the confusion, he stumbled against the deadfall and the raccoon, seizing the opportunity, fled.

I wanted to laugh. I would have liked to get a fat coon for the pot, but our food supply was ample, so perhaps the lesson was well learned, for I knew that Tim would be more careful in the future. 'Maybe you should have used your club,' I said.

'Yes,' he said. 'I will next time.'

Over the days, his snares caught two rabbits, but the deadfall never claimed another victim. My ankle healed, and although it sounds boastful, my camp cooking improved tremendously. I scoured the woods for additions to the pot, and discovered many. The most useful find was a patch of rose hips, which remain on the wild rose bushes even after a hard frost. I had heard Miss Pauline mention their nourishing qualities, but what she didn't say was that they also tasted good. They were well protected by brambles. Gathering them was an adventure in itself, but the results were worth the effort. We ate them boiled with a little stew gravy for flavour. Eaten raw, they were like dried apples, which is the way we liked them best. I sent Tim to gather as many as he could find, since they would be a welcome addition to our travelling rations once we could move again.

One afternoon, after he had been ranging in a larger circle around camp than usual, Tim came home with startling news.

'I found a banana tree,' he declared.

I pooh-poohed his statement. 'We are too far north for banana trees. They grow only in the tropical rain forest.'

Triumphantly he produced his booty. 'Then what is this?'

I took what he offered, which *did* resemble a short, squat, green banana. I sniffed at it. The odour was fragrant and cloying.

'Where did you get this?' I asked.

'There's a clearing about half a mile down the hill,' he said. 'I found this under a tall, skinny tree growing there. There were some more on the ground, but they had turned black.'

I peeled back the hide. The fruit within was pale yellow. I tasted a morsel. It was sweet, unlike anything I had ever eaten. I could not tell whether I liked it or not, but of course that was no consideration.

'I think it's a custard apple,' I said. 'I remember hearing about them in school. The Lewis and Clark expedition came across them on their homeward trail and found them tasty. Some people call them pawpaws.'

Tim tasted the pawpaw and made a face. 'I don't like it.'

'You will cultivate a taste,' I said. 'Were there green ones up in the tree?'

'I think so. I saw clusters of something there.'

'We'll have to gather some green ones, as well as the ripe ones on the ground. Then we'll have a supply that will last for weeks.'

Our most precious find, however, was the beechnuts. Mindful of my father's admonition to seek fat at every opportunity I remembered that nuts were rich in essential oil, which was the same thing. We kept our eyes peeled for walnuts, hickory nuts, even acorns, and found a few. But the squirrels had beaten us to most of those. It was Tim's discovery of a small grove of beech trees that gave us our first ample supply of nuts. The trees were almost a mile from camp, so I didn't go there until near the end of our stay. But one morning, when we had waked to find the ground and tree branches covered with glistening white frost, Tim set off on his morning hunt and returned with his pockets crammed with soft round burrs. They were easily opened. Within were two heart-shaped brown nut morsels.

'The frost must have brought them down,' Tim said, 'I went by there yesterday and didn't notice a single nut.'

'Are there more?' I asked.

'Hundreds. But the birds and the squirrels are already at work.'

I gave him my extra shirt. 'Use this as a sack. Fill it up as fast as you can. Those nuts on the ground will not last long. Hurry!'

He departed, and I limped off to gather pigweed for soup.

Yes, for the time we lived at the spring in the forest, we had nothing to complain about in the way of food.

The day came when I felt strong enough to keep up with Tim, and it was none too soon. Every night had been colder than the last, and twice there had been light sprinkles of powder snow, sifting down through the tall pines. Winter was knocking on our door.

I was not afraid of travelling in snow, though if it gets deep, it can be exhausting work breaking your trail through it. But it would be dangerous on the trail if we should be hit by a blizzard, which was not unknown in those parts in November. Although I assured Tim that my ankle was as good as new, it was still tender. If I stepped carelessly, it was apt to catch.

We had sufficient supplies for several days. I had dried two or three pounds of the turkey by cooking it very slowly to make a sort of jerky. We had at least a pound of shelled beechnuts. I had hoarded enough beans to make two or three small meals. There were two small partridges, roasted whole over the fire and one lonely snowshoe rabbit caught the last night in one of Tim's snares.

He had gone around that last morning checking them and removing the twine in case we needed it later. Also, it would have been cruel to leave an unattended snare to kill a rabbit once we were gone.

I now had my own knife. It had begun life as a humble table knife which had been in our utensils. In my idle moments at the camp, I had rubbed it for hours against a smooth stone, and now it held an edge which, while my father could not have shaved with it, was sufficient for slicing meat. It was my idea to divide supplies and gear as equally as possible between the two of us, so that if one pack should be lost, we would have enough remaining in the other for survival.

We didn't hurry nor did we dawdle. Our course, as before, was southeast. On the first day I would guess that we made five or six miles easily. We stopped often and listened, for sound carries far. If someone was in the woods with us, we might have been able to hear him. But all we heard was one itchy buck crashing off through the underbrush when we surprised him feeding on some wild apples. We thanked him for pointing them out to us and gathered all we could carry easily. I warned Tim against gorging himself on them raw, for they can produce a mighty stomach ache. He ate one, complaining of its bitterness. I chewed on a bit of one and agreed. Cooked down, though, they would be tasty.

Our path seemed to be more downhill than up. I expressed the hope that we were working our way out of the mountains. Tim didn't answer, but I knew what he was thinking. It was a foolish thing to have said, since I knew better than he how many mountains still surrounded us.

We stopped late in the afternoon, and none too soon, for my ankle was beginning to throb. There was an oppressiveness about the air that disturbed me. 'I wonder if we are brewing up to a storm?' I said.

Tim studied the sky – what he could see of it through the trees. 'It looks clear,' he said.

When the fire got properly started, its smoke did not rise briskly as usual, but hung down around the ground in slow-moving clouds.

'Well,' said Tim. 'I'm afraid you might be right. See how the smoke's behaving? Dad said that's a sure sign of rain.'

'Or snow. We may be in for a snowstorm.'

On the chance that the campfire was correct, we spent

94

extra time building a stronger lean-to than usual and made sure we had enough firewood for more than one night. Instead of wasting time cooking, we ate ravenously of the roasted partridge and kept at our work until darkness made it impossible to move safely out of range of the campfire's light.

I peeled some of the wild apples and put them on the fire to boil down to apple sauce, which would be good the next morning. Neither of us was sleepy, so we sat at the edge of the lean-to and talked.

'Do you think we'll ever get home, Lizzy?'

'Of course I do. Don't tell me you doubt it?'

'Sometimes I get scared.'

'I don't blame you. Only a fool wouldn't be scared. But there's nothing wrong with being afraid. It's only when you are so afraid that you can't act that it's wrong. Otherwise, I think a little fear is a good thing. It keeps us from behaving too rashly and makes us think before stepping. Had I been a little more afraid of that log, I wouldn't have slipped and sprained my ankle.'

'I guess my mother is worried about us,' Tim said.

This was the first time in quite a while I had even thought about Miss Pauline. Why, of course she was worried half-sick with despair, no doubt. We were long over-due. If the searchers went to look for us where my father told Indian Pete we were going, they would have no luck, for we were not, and had never been, there.

'She'll be all right,' I told Tim. 'Miss Pauline is a tough old bird.'

To my surprise, he broke out in tears.

'You take that back!' he shouted.

'Why, Tim,' I said, 'I meant it as a compliment.'

'She's my mother,' he said. 'You can't call her an old bird.'

Hastily I said, 'I take it back. Honour bright.'

Still sniffling, he said: 'I know you never liked her. Or me either.'

I started to answer, then held my tongue. This would have to be said carefully, for I did not want to lie nor did I want to hurt his feelings.

'That's not so,' I said slowly. 'But blood is blood, Tim. You feel more for your natural mother than you ever could for your stepfather, and that's only right. Well, it's the same for me only turned around. But – and I would not lie – I do like Miss Pauline very much, and even though you irk me at times, if I am forced to admit it, I will confess to liking you too.'

He rubbed his nose with his sleeve. 'Really?'

'Three owlhoots and a churchyard bell,' I said. That was our strongest oath, and it satisfied him.

'Lizzy?' he said after a while.

'What, Tim?'

'What do you mean to do when we get home?'

'Do?'

'I guess we'll have to go right to school, won't we? We'll have a lot of absences to make up.'

I shook my head. 'I'm not going back to school, not right off,' I told him. 'There's work to do.'

'What kind of work?'

'Indian Pete and me are going to find that road where the Model T is and go down the creek and fetch out my father.'

He didn't answer for a long time, and when he did, his voice had a bad crack in it. 'Oh,' he said. Then: 'I want to go with you.'

'You can go, Tim. I promise you that.'

He burrowed under the blankets. 'I'm sleepy. Lizzy, will you tell me a story?'

'Yes,' I said, and I told him the first part of Sinbad the Sailor, which was one of his favourites, until he was asleep. Then I sat and stared into the fire and hoped that it would not snow hard.

In the morning the air was heavy and the branches drooped under the cracking frost, but there was no snow. We looked longingly at the firewood we had gathered so laboriously the previous evening, but there was no way to take it with us. The cooked apples were frozen in the pot. While Tim packed up our gear, I melted them over the dying embers of the fire, and we ate them for breakfast. They would have benefited from a little sugar and nutmeg but were still a welcome change from stew.

The air grew more chill as the day wore on. By midafternoon we both knew that we were in for a storm. We had lived in the mountains too long to mistake the omens.

We were just about to make early camp when Tim stiffened and said: 'Look!' He pointed downhill, through the trees. 'I see water.'

I craned my neck but could see nothing. Although he was a year younger, Tim was four inches taller than me. 'Come on,' he said, hurrying downhill. I followed, and it was then that the snow began to come through the trees, powder snow at first, then larger flakes, clinging to our glistening cheeks.

Halfway to the lake I saw it. The water was deep blue. We made our way towards it, changing our course slightly to the east to do so. It had been not more than half a mile away when Tim spotted it, so before long we were on its shores and looking across, searching the opposite bank for houses or boats in the water. We saw nothing but dead white trees in the water where the water had risen and killed them, and the dark green of the pines beyond.

Disappointed, Tim said: 'Well, at least we'll have plenty of fresh water. Maybe we can catch some fish.'

We skirted the shore for a few hundred yards until we came on a suitable camp site. As I unpacked the gear, Tim gathered the limbs for the lean-to. The snow was coming down heavily now, and we worked as fast as we could.

We finished in time. When the fire was blazing, I made some hot spruce tea and then began cooking up some beans which we had not had for some time, sweetening them with the leftover partridge and rabbit. Meanwhile Tim gathered and broke up firewood which we used to block one end of the lean-to. I piled some logs behind the fire to act as a reflector, and before long we were cosy and comfortable. Once you've done a task long enough, it becomes automatic and second nature.

'I think we're in for it,' Tim said, staring up at the darkening sky, now filled with snow.

'We'll be snug and safe,' I promised, stirring the beans. 'And the snow will make it easier to find rabbit trails – perhaps even deer. Think you could hit a deer with that revolver?'

He grinned. 'After our friend the raccoon, I wouldn't bet on it.'

We ate and turned in early. The snow whispered through the spruce boughs, and some sifted through and misted our blankets. But as I had promised, we were warm and dry.

The storm blew throughout the night and was still going strong when dawn came. We looked out at the drifts but made no move to get up. The fire was out. It would be a cold, wet job rekindling it.

'Who needs a fire?' Tim said. 'I'm warm.'

'You may be right. Let it go until we need it for cooking. We can eat beechnuts for breakfast.'

The day wore on, but the storm did not abate. We talked quietly of unrelated things, such as our favourite kinds of pie. Mine was blackberry, while Tim was inclined towards peach. I pointed out that since peaches would not grow in our climate, the only ones he was familiar with came in cans. He agreed, but still preferred them. As for ice-cream, we had eaten only chocolate and vanilla and liked both.

'If only we had some condensed milk and sugar now,' I said, scooping up a handful of fresh snow. 'I could make snow cream.'

'That *would* be good.'

We watched the snow for a while.

'I have read,' I said, 'that of all the trillions and trillions of snowflakes, no two are alike.'

'Aw,' Tim said. 'They're just flakes, aren't they?'

'Under the microscope they have very complicated designs.'

'How would you put a snowflake under a microscope?' he scoffed. 'It'd melt.'

98

'Maybe they keep the microscope in an ice box,' I said. 'Or they might take it outside.'

He scooped up some snow and looked at it. It melted in his hand. 'Snow is just frozen water,' he said, 'and it's all the same.'

The snow came down all day and on into the night. We had to get up during the afternoon and start a fire and shove some of the snow back from the entrance to our shelter. I packed the pot with snow and melted it down. It was amazing how a whole pot of snow became only an inch or so of water. When I had melted enough, I put in some of the turkey and the frozen, leftover beans. Meanwhile Tim plunged through the drifts and came back with enough spruce needles for tea, which we started in the other pot.

'I don't even like regular tea,' he grumbled. But I noticed that he drank his share when it was ready. We had to use the same tin cup as it was the only one left.

We had both lost weight by then, I'm sure, but I do not think it was an unhealthy loss. Aside from my injury, we were vigorous and hearty. We had been prone to minor stomach cramps, probably from the high proportion of wild meat in our diet. And we both suffered from constipation. Other than that, we fared better in those northern forests living off the land than I have heard the children of our city slums do, living in their own homes.

The snow continued. We lazed away the rest of the second day and evening. It was late that night that I noticed that the steady rustle of the snowfall had stopped. I got up and put more wood on the fire. As it blazed up, I happened to look out into the night.

I screamed. Tim leaped up and hurried out.

'What is it?' he said.

I pointed, but there was nothing.

'What did you see?'

'Two red eyes looking at me.'

'Oh, is that all?'

'They were horrible.'

'It was probably just a deer. The fire shines on their

99

eyes, just like the reflectors on the back of the Model T. Have you ever noticed?'

I could not honestly say that I had. It was enough to give a person a fright, I can tell you. I went back to bed trembling. When I fell asleep it was to dream of being chased by an old automobile with blazing red eyes for headlights.

The wind rose, and the snow began to come down again. Several times we had to push it back from the entrance to our shelter. The branches and thatch shook with every gust. Hours passed, and we were both hungry, but twice Tim lost matches trying to start a fire, so we gave up and gnawed on the few cooked rations we had left.

When day came, it was dark and overcast and the air was filled with swirling snow.

'I think we're in a blizzard,' said Tim.

'It will blow over,' I said. But inside, I was terrified. I knew that such storms could last for days. If this one did, we were in trouble. We could be frozen to death. We huddled together and tried to cheer each other up.

'You're not a bad chum, for a girl,' Tim said. But I started crying, thinking of my father and of all the dangers we had faced and yet had to face.

When the wind let up a little, Tim said, 'Maybe I can find some dry wood.'

'You stay right here,' I said. 'If you got out in that storm, you'll get turned around and I'll never see you again.'

The day passed slowly and night came. Only the wind increased. Perhaps the heavy snowfall helped us, for as it piled up around our shelter it helped to cut the wind. But it was cold; and closely as Tim and I huddled in our blankets, we were still chilled to the bone. I don't think either of us got much sleep that night.

There was nothing we could do but wait and hope. If the storm blew itself out before we were too far gone, we might be able to dig out and set up a livable camp or find a way across the nearby lake. If it went on too long, we would either die or else be so weak that we could not forage for ourselves afterwards.

Near dawn, it seemed as if the howl of the wind died somewhat, and I dozed a little.

When I woke the sun was shining. Somehow Tim had managed to get a tiny fire going and was melting snow in a pot.

'The storm is over,' he said.

'Good, maybe you can get –'

'Some spruce needles,' he said, grinning. 'I already did.'

I leaned forward and impulsively kissed his cheek. He made a groaning sound, but I could tell that he was pleased.

We made tea and got warm. It was one of the best mornings during that ordeal.

Late in the morning we plunged out into the snow to take our bearings. It was about two feet deep, except where it had drifted, piled by the wind into huge slopes that were shoulder high. It was hard going. I despaired of setting out on our trail again and forcing our way through the drifts.

Tim, meanwhile, had climbed up to a small ridge where he stopped and stood, looking down towards the lake. He turned and waved to me.

'Lizzy! Come up here!'

I plunged through the waist-high drifts and joined him. Silently he pointed.

A hundred yards away, nestled against the protecting hill, facing the lake, was a small log cabin.

The door wasn't even locked. There was a hasp, but only a forked stick held it closed. We pried the heavy door open and peered inside.

The room, which was small, had two bunks at one end. A pot-bellied stove was in the centre. A pipe, supported by baling wire, was suspended across the room. There were three windows, both shuttered. The shadows were dark and gloomy.

I was furious. 'We should have looked farther! I was

stupid! We lay there in the snow all that time and nearly died while the cabin was right here!'

'You couldn't have known,' Tim said. He found, now that his eyes were accustomed to the gloom, a kerosene lantern which was almost full. He struck a match, lit it, and we were able to see, in the pale yellow light, the treasure trove we had stumbled on to.

There were blankets and tools – an axe, a saw, even an awl, were piled in a heap near the door. Shelves which ringed the room were piled with canned goods and boxes of staple goods. One wall was almost completely covered with stretched hides. Tim examined them. 'These are this year's catch,' he said. 'This is a trapper's cabin.'

'Where is he?' I asked.

'Maybe the storm caught him out on his line, and he's waiting it out. Or he may have taken a load down to the buyers.'

I looked around. It was all too much for me, and I began to cry. Tim looked away. 'Come on, come on.'

'Look!' I cried. 'There's sugar, ten whole pounds. And salt. And flour.'

'It doesn't belong to us,' he pointed out.

'No; we'll pay for everything we use. The trapper is bound to be back today or tomorrow, and he can help us get home. Tim, we don't have to go back in the woods any more!'

I saw that realisation dawn in his eyes.

'You start a fire,' he said. 'I'll go and get our gear.'

He left, and I opened the stove door. There was a fire already laid, with kindling and twisted birch bark. One strike of a match and in minutes the flames were dancing. I closed the flue halfway so as not to send all our heat up the stove pipe, and began to look around again.

Whoever lived there was a large man. Near one of the bunks there was a boot into which I could have put both my feet. He was a neat man, too. The cabin was spick and span. All of his clothes were hung neatly on nails. The cabin was snug; all of the chinks had been filled in with moss and mud. I opened the cupboard and found plates and knives and forks. There was a large, black skillet hanging on one wall and near it two pots and a square pan for baking bread. The canned goods were mostly fruit. Our host apparently lived off the land, except for something to stuff his sweet tooth with. There was a large bag of dried beans and another with dried green peas. I immediately put some of them in a pot and went out and filled it with snow, then put it on the stove to melt. Green pea soup would be a welcome change.

Tim returned, carrying our blankets and the food bag. He was gasping for breath.

'Sit down, Tim.'

'No, I'll go back for the rest. The wind's coming up. The snow's drifting again.'

He was right, so I didn't argue. I continued my inventory of the cabin. There was a single-barrel shotgun hanging from two nails but no shells. I found two empty cases for 12-gauge shells, red cardboard tubes, but they had already been fired. I sniffed at them; I have always liked the smell of gunpowder.

An old apple crate under one of the bunks was filled with steel traps, small ones used for muskrat and beaver. There were stretching boards hand-carved from soft pine. In another box, wrapped in oiled paper, I came across a handsome hunting-knife. It was razor sharp. I wrapped it up again and put it back. The trapper would not be pleased to learn that we had been fingering through all his possessions. He could not begrudge us the few provisions we ate, or the firewood we burned, for the law of the woods says that your cabin should offer sanctuary to those who are lost. It was our obligation not to steal his valuables or do malicious damage.

I found some Mason jars. To my joy, one contained cakes of dried yeast. I would be able to make bread, or at least biscuits. There was no butter, but a can of lard was about half full. I found two pounds of coffee beans and near them, five large cans of condensed milk. I would be able to make milk gravy to go with the turkey! It was enough to set me off to sniffling again.

Naturally, that is the moment Tim returned with the rest of our gear. He gave me a disgusted look, and set about unpacking the hastily tied bundles. He and I hung the damp blankets over a rope that stretched from one end of the cabin to the other and added our soggy outer clothing. The chill was gone from the room now, and we could be comfortable in just our shirts and jeans.

'There's a rack of at least twenty cords of firewood outside,' Tim told me. 'The trapper must plan to spend the winter here.'

'Maybe he'll see the smoke from the chimney and come to see what's up,' I said.

'He won't get mad at us, will he?'

'I don't think so,' I said. 'From the way he lives, I would say that he is a careful and prudent man. He'll understand our predicament.'

Tim looked around. 'It's nice to be inside.'

I had been thinking the same thing. The walls were somehow confining, though, used as we were to letting our eyes seek the horizon.

'Did you see anything to carry water in?' I asked. It was no fun melting snow. The effort involved was more than the result was worth.

'There's a bucket outside,' he said.

'Take it to the lake and fill it,' I told him. 'We'll keep it near the fire, so it won't freeze.'

While he was gone, I located the coffee pot. We would put it on the stove, to provide moisture in the air and a constant supply of hot water.

Tim came back with some water, and I filled the coffee pot, then added some more to the pea soup which was cooking down. 'Is there coal oil outside for the lamp?'

'I didn't see any,' Tim said. 'But there's a shed I didn't check.'

'Go check it. We don't want to burn up all of the man's fuel for his lamp.'

While he was doing that, I opened one of the cans of milk. It was half frozen. I made a mental note to heat any cans near the fire before opening them, although if we kept the cabin warm they should all thaw gradually. I was able to shake out enough milk to mix with water, however, and I put half of the white liquid aside for gravy and mixed the rest with some flour into which I had crumbled a bit of yeast. I rolled the dough out until it was tough and rubbery, and then pounded it several times and put it near the stove to rise.

I took the strips of cooked turkey and put them in the milk mixture. While they were soaking, I put some lard in the big frying-pan and set it on top of the stove. Soon the air was filled with the pungent aroma of hot grease.

Tim came in and said, excitedly, 'You'll never guess what's in that shed!'

'Coal oil?'

'Gallons. A big drum so heavy I can't budge it. But there's snow shoes and all kinds of winter stuff. Ice runners. He must bring his supplies over the lake in the wintertime, by sled.'

'We will ask him when he returns. But surely that's not why you're so excited.'

He shook his head. 'There's a big buck hanging there. He's frozen stiff, but except for the heart and liver, which have been taken, he's completely whole. There must be a hundred pounds of meat there. And there are boxes of vegetables, down in a hole and covered with sod. Turnips and potatoes and onions.'

Potatoes! Onions! I am able to live without ever seeing another turnip, but that is a matter of taste. I told Tim to get us two large potatoes and a big onion. What a feast we would have! I hoped the trapper would return just as it was ready. What better demonstration of our gratitude than to serve him a piping hot meal as fine as he could get in any restaurant?

I put Tim to peeling the vegetables while I attacked the bread dough again. It had risen to almost double its original volume and was ready for the pan. The stove did not have an oven, but I could cover the bread pan and use it like a Dutch oven. I greased it and shaped biscuits with my hands, placing them half an inch apart in the bottom. I left the pan near the heat to rise again and applied myself to the turkey, which had soaked up the milk mixture and was soft again. I put it in the frying-pan. The sizzling brought Tim's head up, and he smiled.

'It's almost like being at home.'

'Slice up those potatoes and let me have them,' I said. He did so, and I put them into the frying pan too. Then I dosed them and the turkey liberally with salt and pepper. It was so good not to have to stint on salt. Our own supply had dwindled down to a mere pinch or two.

Then I put the biscuits on to bake. Soon the odour of their fresh dough filled the room.

'Oh boy!' Tim said.

I cut up the onion and put it in the frying-pan, and then covered everything. I reminded myself to keep a wary eye on it to avoid burning.

'Tim,' I said with mock sternness, 'where are the spruce needles?'

He had stood up and started out the door before he saw that I was joking, and he began to laugh. I said: 'No, we'll forgo the spruce tea tonight in favour of some coffee and milk. How's that?'

'Oh yes.' I gave him a dozen coffee beans to pound into powder, which he did, wrapping them in a bit of cloth and hitting them with the flat side of the trapper's axe. When they were done, I put them into the coffee pot, where the water was steaming nicely. Another delicious odour wafted through the cabin, I closed my eyes. Tim had been right: it *was* almost like being home.

I looked at the biscuits which were coming along nicely. 'If only we had some butter,' I said ungratefully. Tim gave me a surprised look, got up, and went out the door.

He was back in a moment, holding a square block wrapped in waxed paper. I stared at it. It was not butter, but the cheap imitation, margarine, which Miss Pauline would not allow in her kitchen and which now appeared more precious than as much gold.

'Where did you find this?'

'Out in the shed. There's two more left. I guess the

trapper put it there to keep it cold.'

The margarine was still soft enough for me to slice off a piece. I broke off a corner and popped it into my mouth. Yes, it tasted like butter and looked like butter, and when it had softened, it would spread like butter. I found myself wondering what Miss Pauline had against it.

'Bring in some firewood, Tim, then we'll eat.'

While he was gone, I added the rest of the milk mixture to the turkey and vegetables and threw in a little flour to thicken it. It smelled like chicken and dumplings. I found two heavy crockery cups without handles and poured the coffee. I used two deep plates for the green pea soup which had simmered down beautifully. I put these luxuries on the table to surprise Tim when he returned and then put the biscuits on the 'hearth' in front of the stove to keep warm. Some of the yellow margarine went into a saucer alongside a can of cherry jam I had found. There were even real salt and pepper shakers made of heavy crystal glass. All we lacked were napkins, but the tails of our shirts had done for almost two weeks and could so continue.

Tim came in with a load of firewood and dumped it into the box near the door. I realized that I had forgotten to save some hot water for washing. Very well – we would eat with dirty hands, which was nothing new either.

I put the can of condensed milk on the table. 'Use plenty of milk in your coffee, Tim,' I warned, 'or it will keep you awake.'

He shook some of the yellowish milk into his cup. 'No fear of that,' he said. 'I am already tuckered out, and it's only mid-afternoon.'

'It's the warmth of the fire,' I said. 'We've gotten used to the chill of the outdoors.'

'Well,' he said, 'I prefer the inside, if it's all the same with you.'

I found a wash pan and poured some water in it to heat and put on the stove; then I sat down to eat with Tim. We gulped down the green pea soup as if we had never eaten anything so good before, although if you want the truth, it sorely needed a chunk of salt pork for flavour. We buttered (or would you say, 'margarined'?) the biscuits and dipped them in the soup and ate and ate. 'Save some room,' I said. 'We have turkey and vegetables coming up.'

'I'm hollow as a tree trunk,' Tim said back. 'Is there any more soup?'

There was, but I wanted to save it for supper. I served up, instead, the rich brew of turkey white meat, and onions and potatoes, simmered in milk gravy. I poured it over a biscuit and put it before Tim, and he fell on it like a starving wolf. I tasted my own, and in all modesty, had to admit that it was a success.

All through the meal, I kept hoping the trapper would turn up. 'Did you see any tracks leading away from the cabin?'

'Not a one,' Tim said. 'And there's no road either, not that I could see. That's why I supposed that he must snake his supplies over the lake once it's frozen. I don't think that he could pack all this stuff in here on his back, or even by mule, over an ordinary foot trail.'

'Did you see a boat in the water?'

'No,' he said. 'But there's a place there where it's been run up on shore, and there's a wooden stake driven in the ground for tying it up.'

'Then he must have gone out on the lake before the storm hit,' I said. 'If he had walked along the shore line, his boat would still be here.'

'Or maybe he went to town with his catch,' Tim said.

'I thought of that. But look,' I indicated the furs drying on the wall. Some were well-cured. 'Those beaver are ready for the market. Why did he leave them? They'd bring eight or nine dollars apiece. No, I believe he went out to run his trap line and holed up until the storm was over.'

'Unless it caught him in the middle of the lake,' said Tim.

I had thought of that, too, but didn't wish to linger on it.

We finished eating and spread the last biscuit with cherry jam and shared it for dessert. Then Tim sighed and said, 'I could stretch out right now and go to sleep.'

'You do that. I'll take care of the dishes, and then I wouldn't be surprised if I didn't catch forty winks myself.'

He was asleep by the time his head hit the pillow. I had to slip his boots off. He moaned in his sleep, and I touched his cheek. 'Shhh,' I said, 'sleep, Timmy.'

Bath time.

We had slept like the dead. I got up sometime later in the evening and blew out the lamp to save coal oil and then tumbled back into my own soft bed with a real cotton mattress, and fell into the depths of dreamless sleep. Both Tim and I were fully clothed, which was just as well, because the fire went out during the night and the cabin was chilled when I woke up at dawn. I saw no point in waking Tim, but he heard me moving about and got up too. He went for water while I got the fire going. I had half-expected to be awakened during the night by the arrival of the cabin's owner, but no one came.

After a breakfast of fried dough and margarine, I informed Tim : 'I can't speak for myself, but now that we're indoors, you smell like a goat. We must both take baths.'

He didn't resist, which surprised me, for Tim has never been one for excessive bath taking. Maybe his own ripeness was getting to him.

I heated water and gave him a scrap of cloth for a wash rag and a bar of yellow soap.

'I'll go outside and look around while you bathe,' I said. 'Call me when you're done. Don't put on the same clothes. We'll wash them later. Your other shirt is a little cleaner than the one you're wearing.'

I bundled up warmly, and as I went out the door, called back : 'Wash all over, Tim. Don't skimp.'

The snow was drifted deep around the cabin in places, while in others, the ground was blown bare by the wind. I went out to the shed and examined its contents. The hanging deer had not been skinned. That would not be an easy job for our trapper host now that it was frozen. But with care, he had an ample supply of meat there. It had been taken out of season, of course.

The box of margarine had originally held four one-pound chunks. Two were missing. Tim had brought one inside. The trapper must have eaten the other.

I went down to the boat landing at the edge of the lake. From there I could see that the lake widened out in both directions. The far shore seemed to be a mile or so away, while there was no visible end to the right. At the left there was a clump of islands which blocked my view.

The wind was chill, and I tucked my hands inside my jacket.

Tim had been right. There was no sign of a trail. Even with the snow, I should have been able to see the signs of a trail. Our trapper arrived and departed by way of the lake, using a boat until the freeze and an ice sled after.

I wished he would come back. From the way the cabin was stocked, he apparently spent quite a bit of time there, which suggested that he did not like to camp out on the trap line. He would probably have arranged it so that he could cover it in a series of one-day trips from the cabin, which is the way Indian Pete preferred to trap also.

Well, if the storm had caught him at the far end of the line, he would have holed up and might be on his way home this morning. The sky was clear, and although the wind was brisk, it did not throw up any whitecaps on the lake, so rowing would be safe.

'Lizzy! I'm through.'

I went back to the cabin. Tim had made a wet mess on the floor near the stove. I would wait until I had bathed too before mopping up. I sent Tim down for some more water after throwing the lukewarm water he had used out the door. While this new water was heating, I suggested that he explore around the cabin some more, particularly for any signs of a trail. I still had hopes that there might be one, since if there was not and if our host did not return, we would have to wait until the lake froze unless we wanted to start walking through the woods again.

When the water was steaming, I took off my clothes and took a quick bath, scrubbing myself with the cloth and the strong yellow soap until my skin turned pink. I got some in my eyes and the stinging was enough to make me howl.

It was at just that moment that Tim burst in, shouting: 'A boat!' then stopped aghast. He backed out quickly. I dried off and threw on my clothes and went to the window.

Yes, there was a boat – far out. But it did not seem to be coming in our direction. That was strange.

I called Tim in and we both watched out of the window. The distant boat appeared to have one man in it, and he was rowing from left to right, perhaps half a mile out. Just as he was about to pass out of sight, he paused in his course, then slowly the boat turned towards the cabin.

'That is very odd,' I said. 'It was as if he were going somewhere else and only at the last moment saw this cabin.'

'Or maybe the smoke from the fire.'

'Well, anyway, help is on the way,' I said. 'Quick, fetch some more water. We must have some hot coffee waiting for our visitor.'

There was plenty of time to brew the coffee, for it took the distant boat some twenty minutes to make shore. He was a large man, wearing a black overcoat which did not seem to be very well suited for the woods. He had a hard time tying up the boat. Obviously he didn't know this landing.

'Tim,' I said, clutching his arm, 'I don't like this. Listen to what I say and agree with everything, no matter how strange it sounds.'

'But I don't – '

'Don't argue!'

I rushed to the door and threw it open just as the man was reaching for the latch.

'Oh,' I said, putting disappointment into my voice. 'We thought you were our daddy.'

Close up, our visitor was not an appealing sight. His

face was covered with a thick beard. It was not a neat, trimmed beard, but the kind a hobo lets run rampant.

The man looked around the cabin. 'Where is your daddy?' he asked.

'He went out this morning to run the trap line,' I said.

Without another word, the man stepped inside, tracking wet snow on my clean floor. 'Alone?' he asked.

I improvised. 'Oh, no. My Uncle Pete was with him. They ought to be back pretty soon if you want to wait.'

He saw the shotgun hanging on the wall and went right over to it. 'Where is the ammunition for this scattergun?'

'There isn't any,' I said.

He scowled. 'Don't lie to me, girl.'

'You shut up talking like that to her!' Tim yelled.

Without even turning, the big man backhanded Tim up against the wall. It hurt, I could tell, but he blinked back the tears.

'What have you got to eat around here?'

'Nothing,' I said.

'You lie to me once more, little lady,' he warned, 'and I'll make you sorry.'

'I meant there's nothing cooked. I had it in mind to fix something up for my father and Uncle Pete. Do you want to wait?'

He scowled at that. 'I ain't got time.' He looked around the room, took a sight on the sack of beans. He shoved it at Tim. 'Take that down and put it in my boat,' he ordered.

'What?' Tim said.

I was shocked too. This stranger was stealing our provisions! He glared at us. 'Damn you, do what I said and right now!'

I nodded at Tim and he took the sack of beans and left. The man rummaged around the shelves, scorning the canned fruit. But he put the flour and sugar aside, and when Tim came back he was forced to carry them down to the boat also. Everything the man touched was either broken or knocked over and spilled. He didn't seem to care how much damage he did. He pawed through our packs. When he came to my father's pistol, his eyes lit up. 'Now this is more like it,' he declared, sticking it down in his belt.

I flew at him. 'You put that back!' I screamed. 'That belonged to my father!'

'Well, if I meet up with your daddy, I'll be sure to see that he gets a look at it,' he answered. He stuffed his pockets with the leftover margarine and a box of matches that had been in the cabin when he arrived. He peered out the window nervously and cursed. Hurrying through the door, he paused to pick up the axe. Then as I watched him through the window, he rushed down to the boat. Tim had been up to something. He ran when the man approached. I was horrified to see the man lift the pistol and take aim, but Tim dived out of sight in the trees, and the man lowered the gun. He looked back up towards the cabin, started to return, changed his mind, and then got in the boat. He rowed off quickly. Trembling, I watched until he had disappeared around the headland. Then I ran outside and called: 'Tim? Where are you?'

He came out of the trees. He was so mad he was crying. 'I'll get him!' he promised. 'Did you see what he did? I'll get him!'

'You're lucky he didn't shoot you,' I said. 'What were you doing?'

'Trying to kick a hole in his boat. I would have done it, too, if he hadn't caught me.'

'Well, he's gone – let us hope, for good.'

'Who was he? Why did you tell him our father was out on the lake?'

'I'm not sure, Tim. Something about him seemed wrong. He didn't know about this cabin. And did you see how he dressed? It was as if he had stepped out of a town instead of the woods. I think he was maybe one of those convicts who escaped a couple of weeks ago. He must have fled into the woods, and he's been living by breaking into cabins. If he'd known we were here alone, I don't know what he might have done. As it is, he only stole a few things and hurried away because he was afraid our "father" would come back soon.'

'He took the pistol. If he comes back, we don't have any way to protect ourselves.'

'It wouldn't have been much help anyway. Neither of us could shoot a man.'

'Don't be too sure of that,' Tim said darkly.

We went back inside and without enthusiasm began cleaning up the mess our unwelcome visitor had left.

Several days passed, and the trapper owner of the cabin did not appear. We watched the lake anxiously every day, not sure whether we wanted to see a boat or not. Our first impulse, after the escaped convict (for that's what we had decided he was) had gone, was to pack as much as we could carry and move back into the woods. But the weather was fierce. Now I knew that somewhere across that lake there was a trail, and I didn't want to return to the trackless wilderness. We decided that one of us would watch the lake at all times. If we saw the convict returning, we would hide in the woods. Naturally this decision was unrealistic, since we soon grew lax at our lookout.

Tim became fascinated with the useless shotgun. He studied it for hours, examining how the hammer struck the percussion cap of the shell, and handled the empty red cardboard tubes so often that I was sure he would wear them out. 'There must be a way to make this thing shoot,' he would say.

Losing the food the convict had stolen was more of an annoyance than a tragedy. We had plenty left. We made a start on the deer by cutting off a hind quarter with the saw and bringing it inside to thaw. Once it had thawed, getting the thick hide off was a tedious and messy job which took almost a whole day. Neither of us had ever skinned so large a creature before, and we did not know where to begin. But eventually the task was completed.

The snares began to produce other meat. Rabbits were plentiful, but I was wary of serving them too often, mindful of the need for red meat with fat. We ate wild greens.

Once we could find no more of them, I took to cooking slim strips of the inner bark of birch trees, which were very bland and so took on the flavour of whatever they were boiled with. We ate sparingly of the vegetables buried in the storehouse which the thief had not discovered.

Several weeks went by, and my birch bark calendar added the dates until it was December. We had settled into an almost effortless routine. Get up, eat, work, eat, go to bed, and start over again in the morning.

We were merely marking time, and both of us knew it. Tim, particularly, was growing impatient.

'Let's walk around the lake,' he said. 'If the trail's there we'll hit it.'

'We can't be sure of that,' I said. 'You don't know how big this lake is. It could stretch for ten miles to either side. And you know how hard it is to walk along the shore line, especially with the deep snow covering up any inlets that might be just barely frozen over. We'd break through for sure.'

So he gave up pestering me on that point and took to studying the shotgun again. He had found several of the .22 cartridges for his gun in his pocket, but, of course, they wouldn't fit the 12-gauge shotgun.

'There ought to be some way to shoot these,' he said. 'If we only had a smaller barrel to put inside the shotgun's big one.'

'Maybe we could make one out of a hollow reed,' I suggested.

He got excited over that and rushed out to pick some reeds from the edge of the lake. But when he tried cutting one to size and fitting it down inside the shotgun it became obvious immediately that it wouldn't work.

'We've got to make this gun shoot,' he declared. 'If it would, I bet I could bag a goose.'

'Flying half a mile up?' I scoffed. 'You're a dreamer.'

'No,' he said. 'They're out on the lake right now.'

I went to the window. He was right. A large flock of geese was drifting just off the boat landing, dipping their heads in the water for food. Several had come up on to the thin ice and were foraging there.

'Do you think they would sit still long enough for us to get close enough to strike one with a stick?' I asked.

'No,' Tim replied. 'I tried to creep up on them and they jumped back in the water.'

'They weren't there yesterday.'

'I think they came in late last night,' he said.

'Not very long. They're late now. I think they're just tired. They'll leave as soon as they get their second wind.'

'How long will they stay?'

I rummaged back through my memory. I remembered my father and Indian Pete telling stories around the fireplace about how they had hunted as boys. One tale had included the trick of catching wild turkeys with the small fence. But I was willing to bet that a goose had more sense than any turkey.

'We'll trap them,' I said suddenly.

'With what?' Tim said. We both looked towards the box under the trapper's bed. What fools we had been! Setting snares and deadfalls when we had a half-dozen of the finest steel traps you could want.

'Do you think we could get them to stick their heads in one of those traps?' I said.

'No,' Tim said. 'But I know where to set them, and maybe we can get us a beaver. Or a coon.'

He stared at me and I stared back. He began to laugh.

'We really are some woodsmen!' I said. 'Why did we let those traps rust under the bed?'

'Well,' said Tim, 'they weren't ours, and I guess I just forgot about them.'

'So did I,' I said, 'and I'm ashamed of it.'

'What about the geese?' he prompted.

Then I remembered a story Indian Pete had told. 'Dig a trench!' I cried.

'A what?'

I led him out, and together we scooped out a trench some two feet wide and four feet deep. The snow was heavily crusted. It was lucky we had the trapper's spade, for it would have been hard going with our bare hands.

It broke my heart to do it, but I took the handful of beans the convict had left unnoticed in our pack and scattered some of them out on the thin ice, then made a path of beans into the trench.

'Now, hide,' I whispered.

We crouched down, out of sight of the lake and the swimming geese. We heard their curious honking but could not see them.

'Is it working?' Time asked.

'Be quiet.'

We waited, trembling, in the cold. Then slowly, a magnificent Canadian goose appeared, waddling up the trail of beans I had strewn. He was followed by a second, smaller bird. I pointed this one out to Tim.

'I'll take the last one,' I said. 'Wait until I give the word, then run for all your might.'

We held our breath, waiting to see if the birds would follow the bait into the trench. They hesitated, and then the first one went in. The other held back.

'The big one's eating all the bait!' Tim said.

'Don't move,' I warned. 'Give them a little more time.'

Slowly, cautiously, the second goose waddled down into the trench. I gave Tim a punch on the leg.

'Go!'

We were upon the surprised geese before they knew what hit them. Part of my plan involved frightening them into trying to fly, so as we came into view, I gave a wild Indian yell, which scared Tim almost as much as it did the geese. It had its effect. The big birds spread their wings – or tried to – there wasn't enough room in the trench for them to take off. They beat helplessly against the frozen walls. Tim jumped into one end, blocking it, and I came in by the rear door, and the birds were trapped.

They did not give up without a fight, however. I knew from my barnyard experience that geese are prone to give little girls a fierce nip with their strong beaks, and these wild birds did not disappoint me.

Tim was trying to grab hold of his goose by the body.

Meanwhile it was giving him what for around his face and ears. 'Get it by the neck!' I shouted. I had my own bird, although it clawed at me with its feet and flapped its wings. I twisted the neck until the head came off and the goose flailed in the snow. I felt a little guilty at letting the blood go to waste, but I had forgotten to bring a string from the cabin, and somehow with the relatively large supply of food we had, the nutritional value of blood no longer seemed as important as it had in the woods.

I heard Tim yell as the goose took another nip at his ear, then he wrung its neck and flung the thrashing carcass away from him. He fell back into the snow, gasping.

Staring out at the lake, I was surprised to see that our struggles had not disturbed the rest of the flock. They had merely drifted a little further out from shore.

'Quick,' I told Tim. 'Let's get these birds up to the cabin.'

Mine was heavy – over ten pounds – and Tim's was even bigger. We were panting as we reached the shed and threw the geese inside.

'What else can we use for bait?' I asked, peering around the shed.

'We've got some beechnuts left,' Tim said. He was right. I had been saving a double handful for trail rations when we began to walk out. But the fat geese were worth more to us.

'Get them.' I hurried back down to the trench and with the spade strengthened its sides where our struggles had knocked them down.

We baited the trap again with the handful of beechnuts. After waiting in the cold for half an hour, our efforts were rewarded by a large goose. Since the bird had come alone, we both jumped out and soon subdued it.

A third attempt to lure the birds ashore failed when darkness came on. I picked up as many of the beechnuts as I could find. 'We can try again in the morning,' I said.

We hung the three geese alongside what remained of the deer carcass. They had already begun to freeze, so there was no chance of their spoiling. Already, visions of thick, greasy soup were dancing in my mind.

Inside, I cleaned the blood off Tim's neck and ear. He had been nicked rather handsomely by the first goose.

'That's a wound of honour,' I told him. 'You'll be able to wear it proudly.'

'You're crazy in the head,' he said, but I could see that he was pleased.

We went to bed early. After I had blown out the lamp, I told him a story for the first time in several nights. It was the first part of the Wizard of Oz. Then we spent some time wondering out loud where Oz was and what would happen to Dorothy and if she ever got home safely again.

The geese were gone in the morning. It was fortunate that we had acted without hesitation. But that is always true in the woods. Never put anything off until tomorrow, for you may be sure that tomorrow will dawn rainy or that the geese will be gone or that the wind will be blowing too hard to fish. If a thing must be done, do it as soon as you think of it; then there will be no regrets.

Tim and I spent part of the morning scraping the piece of deer hide that had come from the rear haunch.

'What are we going to do with this?' he asked.

'Nothing, I hope,' I answered.

He worked in silence for a while. Then he said, 'In that case, why are we scraping off the hair?'

'Because, if things go wrong, we may have to eat this deerskin.'

He laughed. 'You are doing it to me again.'

'Didn't you ever hear of starving men eating their shoes?'

'Yes, but we're not starving.'

'I hope that we never *will* be. But if it comes to that, rawhide is very good food, although mighty hard to chew. On the other hand, it will do no good to eat your shoes, according to Indian Pete, for the process of tanning destroys all the food value. But a piece of natural hide such as this is as high in protein as the meat it covered.'

'You couldn't get a tooth into it,' Tim said.

'We would cut it into small pieces and boil it as long as we could,' I said. 'If we couldn't do that, we'd take even smaller pieces and chew them until our jaws got tired, and then swallow them whole.'

'In that case, why chew?' he asked. 'Why not just gulp them down?'

'I'm not sure,' I replied. 'Maybe it's because the chewing would help relieve our hunger pangs, or perhaps there is something in our saliva that benefits the food.'

'Go away,' he said. 'You're making me ill.'

Our meal that day was to be a fish chowder I was making from a small northern pike Tim had found on his night line. These skinny, eel-like fish are very bony and have a strong flavour. But they're fatty and greasy, which was why I had used even the head in the chowder. I decided not to mention the head to Tim. I would dispose of the bones after the meat had been cooked off them, and he would never know the difference.

That day, December 6, was when we heard the loud cracking noises outside and rushed out, fearing that our convict had returned and was shooting at us. But it was only the deep freeze gripping green saplings and splitting them with a loud report that was like a gunshot.

My father's prediction that this would be the worst winter in memory was being fulfilled. It had become harder and harder to keep the cabin comfortable, and Tim and I now spent as much time searching for tiny drafts and chinking them up as we did at any other task. Even so, when we got up in the morning the water in the bucket was frozen all the way to the bottom, and it was agony to put our feet on to the cold floor.

There wasn't much snow yet. The first storm had been the only major source of snow. In fact, we would have been better off with more of it. Snow on the top and sides of the cabin, for instance, would have insulated it and permitted comfort with far less expenditure of precious firewood. I was quite worried about the way the stack of wood was diminishing. The trapper must have intended to cut some more, for he could never have got through the entire winter with the supply on hand. When possible, we cut fresh wood rather than use that in the rack, because if the snow ever did arrive, it would become almost impossible to find new wood, and we would be forced to burn that which had already been cut.

There was no thermometer in the cabin, but from the way the cold gripped us the second we ventured outdoors, numbing ears and freezing tears on our cheeks, it must have been below zero, and even colder at night. When going to bed, we sealed every window and stuffed a blanket across the bottom of the door to keep out drafts.

It was this that came closer to killing us than any other hazard.

Neither of us had any warning symptoms. That particular night, we went to bed later than usual. The air had been still and quiet outside, so the fire was not drawing hard. I banked it carefully, adding green wood and closing the damper. With luck, it might keep the cabin warm enough to prevent freezing.

My dreams that night were frightening. I slept restlessly. Instead of being cold, I felt sweaty and feverish. I dreamed of my mother and of Miss Pauline and of my father who looked up at me from that cold hole in the ground and told me quietly, 'You have been a bad girl.' There were probably a dozen other nightmares I can't remember now. It was still dark when I got up. I was gripped by an overwhelming anxiety. I wanted light. I fumbled for the lamp and knocked off its globe. Luckily, it fell on my shirt which was folded on the table alongside it and did not break. I struck a match. Its flame seemed pale and far away. My hand trembled as I applied it to the wick. It didn't flare up as usual. Was the lamp out of coal oil? But then the flame grew slowly, although it did not fill the corners of the room when I put the globe on again.

My head ached heavily. I felt dizzy. Could I have come down with a fever? There was no way to know what time it was. I had an overpowering urge to run outside and throw myself into the snow. It frightened me.

'Tim!' I called.

Without warning, I had to sit down, right on the floor. My legs just went out from under me. My head swam, and I was very close to fainting.

'TIM!'

But he did not stir. It was then that I knew that things were very wrong.

Air! *We were being suffocated by carbon monoxide.* We had done such a good job of sealing the cabin that now the fire in the stove had consumed all the oxygen.

Painfully, I crawled to the door. I could not reach the hasp of the latch. I lay there, sobbing. Why would Tim not come to help? Maybe he was already dead. I knew I had to get that door open, but there was no strength left.

'Please, God,' I whispered. 'Help me!'

It was the first time I had prayed since burying my father. I do not say that it was this prayer which gave me the last flare of energy that got me up on my knees and guided my hand to the latch. But somehow I found the strength, and the door flew open and the freezing wind lashed into the cabin. I fell back gasping for breath. It must have been several minutes before I moved again, because when I was able to struggle to my feet, I was covered with powdered snow.

I rushed over to Tim. I shook him. 'Tim! Wake up! Please wake up!'

He stirred. Thank God, he was alive!

I half-dragged, half-guided his stumbling figure over to the door. He leaned against it, gasping. Slowly, he came awake.

'Hey!' he yelled. 'Why are we standing in the snow?'

He moved to close the door. 'Leave it open,' I said.

'But we'll freeze.'

'No we won't,' I said. I went over to the stove. Yes, the flue draft was completely closed. The fire had burned slowly during the night feeding on the oxygen in the room instead of that which should have been drawn in through the stovepipe. There were still embers in the firebed. I added two small logs and made sure this time that the flue draft was half-open.

I told Tim to close the door. When he came over to warm himself, I said: 'We must always leave a window open a little. We were almost killed tonight by carbon monoxide.'

We had both heard of campers who, taking a heater into their closed tents or into a cave, had perished. But it had never occurred to us that there was any danger in a large cabin. Needless to say, from that night on, we were always sure to have ample ventilation at night.

It may have been this partially opened window that caused us our first real trouble with our animal neighbours in the woods.

Tim and I were out running our small trap line together. It was a dark, cloudy morning. It looked like another storm was coming, and we wanted to be prepared. We found two squirrels in a set of special snares he had built against a tall oak tree.

'I found cuttings under this tree last time,' he said proudly. 'And I knew there was a family of squirrels up there, working away on the late acorns. So look what I did.'

He showed me a sapling he had leaned up against the tree like a runway.

'I don't care what you say,' Tim began. 'Squirrels are just as lazy as any other critter. So if they find an easy way, like up this sapling, they'll take it instead of climbing straight up the side of the tree.'

He had laid several small nooses along the top of the sapling, with their loops held up by tiny branches. Two squirrels had run into the nooses and, once the string closed, fallen off and strangled. Apparently their dangling there did not disturb the other rodents, because when we approached, another one had been in the process of running up the sapling.

They were both grey squirrels, which are larger than the red ones. They make delicious eating. The flavour is nut-like, and the meat is lean. When fried with biscuits and white gravy, there are few dishes that equal them. That was another black mark against the convict. By stealing our flour he had deprived us of biscuits and bread. Even gravy was hard to make without flour to thicken it.

Tim stuffed the squirrels inside his coat and reset the snares. Then we moved on to the next trap.

Altogether, we found a rabbit, another squirrel and a very angry black and white skunk which had been caught about the middle of one of the snares. Tim was very disturbed by his catch.

'I'd let him go,' he said, 'but he'll get me.'

'Well, you can't leave him there,' I said.

'Oh no? Then you release him.'

My bluff having been called, I took Tim's knife. It would do no good just to cut the snare free of its stake, for then the skunk would be trailing a piece of cord which might only trap him somewhere else. It would have to be removed from his body.

I tried to remember what I had heard about skunks. They were very brave. With their formidable weapon, they could afford to be. I had a vague memory of one boy who, having been sprayed, was bathed in gasoline (which did not help) and finally had to be scrubbed down with tomato juice. He had all his hair cut off, too. We had neither gasoline nor tomato juice, and I had no desire to be bald. But I had painted myself into a corner.

My only hope was to avoid alarming the skunk. I spoke softly to him, as I approached.

'No one wants to hurt you, Skunkie dear,' I cooed. 'I only want to help you. Please don't spray me. I'm a friend.'

At least he let me approach without turning on me, but his expression was none too friendly.

'Skunkie dear,' I told him, 'what I am going to do is slip this knife inside that twine and cut you free. I am not going to harm you, so please stay quiet.'

He raised up and for a moment I was afraid he was going to bite me. I kept on talking. I do not remember what I said. Unfortunately, Tim does. He spent many an evening after that, chirping suddenly from the darkness, 'Oh, Skunkie dear, I am your true friend; please do not spray me.' It would take a threat of a cup of cold water over Tim's head to shut him up.

Whatever I said worked, for the skunk did not bite me, nor did he turn his tail towards me. I cut the cord and fled for my life, Tim's laughter ringing in my ears. But I had my revenge. I made him go back and tie the snare up again, and he did so shaking in his boots for fear that the skunk might be lurking under a bush.

We had learned not to blunder the trail, staring at our boots, as many tenderfeet do. There was much to be learned by scanning the treetops for nesting birds and through the forest, for while there was no hope of coming up on a sleeping deer, we did learn their location and frequent haunts that way. It was at such time that Tim bemoaned the lack of a gun. He tried to make a snare large enough to hold a deer, but he had to use a length of rope from the trapper's shed, and it was so visible that it would have taken a stone-blind deer to wander into it.

We saw no more game that day, however. I picked some tender spruce needles. I insisted that we drink spruce tea at least once a day, for I still had a fear of scurvy. And I was always on the lookout for a new plant or tree that might provide a fresh source of food. There was one, in particular, that I sought – the common chickweed, which grows everywhere and flowers once a month. I was sure that it must flourish along the shores of our lake, but the snow had hidden it. Chickweed survives the coldest winter and blooms in the ice. It has numerous tiny seeds which can be dried and eaten. The oval leaves are delicious if you can add some salt and a little butter, and we had both, or at least salt and margarine. Besides, crushed chickweed leaves make a fine poultice which relieves skin rashes and bruises. Our cabin at home was surrounded by it, and it was a fine source of irritation to me that I could find none here.

Before we went back to the cabin, we cut fresh young

strips of inner bark from a birch tree. I intended to slice them very thin and serve them up as a kind of spaghetti. It would be a welcome change from frozen pigweed.

As we approached, we could see that the cabin door was open. We stopped.

'It's the convict!' Tim said.

'But why is the door open?'

'He's stealing the rest of our supplies.'

We hid and watched. After ten minutes or so, without seeing anyone move, I said, 'Well, he must be gone. He wouldn't leave the door open like that if he was on the inside.'

'You stay here,' said Tim. 'I'll sneak up and look in the window.'

He crept through the snow, staying out of the line of the door and windows so if anyone were inside watching, he couldn't be seen. He had to stand on tiptoe to peer in the rear window. He stayed there for a moment, stiff, then turned to me and waved.

He met me near the door. 'It's awful,' he said.

'What's awful?'

He pointed inside. Now that we were near, I could see that the door had been torn off its hinges. Inside, the cabin was a shambles. Our supplies and clothing were strewn everywhere. The stove pipe had been knocked down; the chairs were overturned.

'What happened?' I cried.

'Bear. He came through the window — see? He must have smelled the stew.'

'But why did he wreck everything?'

'Looking for more food.' Tim had a sudden thought and ran out the door, returning quickly. 'It's good the shed door was latched. He didn't get in there.'

Sick at heart, we began cleaning up. The damage looked worse than it was. The bear had eaten everything he could find, but apart from the stew I had been cooking and some slices of venison thawing, there was nothing fresh in the cabin. He had ignored the canned goods.

The fire was out, so Tim rekindled it after we replaced

the stove pipe in its socket. 'Lucky the place didn't catch fire,' he said.

The worse damage was to the window facing the lake. It had been smashed in. There was no repairing it. Tim found some rough planks in the shed, and he pulled a couple of nails out of the walls and boarded it up. This took away our favourite view, as well as preventing us from keeping a lookout across the lake.

I had Tim clean the squirrels and we ate them fried with potatoes that evening.

'It seems like we've been living here for ever,' he said thoughfully, as I washed the dishes.

'We'll be able to leave soon,' I said. 'Once the ice freezes on the lake, we're only a few days from home.'

He looked down at the table. His lips moved. I could not hear the words, but I knew he had repeated: 'Home . . .'

We were awakened by a heavy pounding. I struck a match and lit the lamp. The door was shuddering under the blows of something outside.

'The bear!' Tim shouted. 'He's trying to get in.'

I ran to the sink and fumbled for the sharp knife. Tim said: 'No, get a pot and spoon.' He took the big pot and my large spoon and began to beat on it like a drum. At the same time, he shouted – Indian war whoops we had learned from Indian Pete. I got the idea and joined in. The pounding on the door hesitated. Then it stopped.

'I think we scared him off,' I said.

Tim only pounded harder. 'Make sure!' he called. So I contributed my share to the din.

Our ears were ringing when we finally stopped.

'I didn't think a bear would come right into a cabin where people were living,' I said.

'This one may be old, or wounded. Lizzy, I've just got to get that shotgun so it'll shoot. The next time, he may not scare so easy.'

'Maybe he's already so scared he won't come back.'

Tim stared at me. 'Don't kid me, Lizzy. Do you want

to take the chance that he'll break in again, whether or not we're here? If he wrecks this cabin and eats up our supplies we'll have to live in the woods again until we can cross the lake. We just can't take the risk.'

'Well, you've got a gun with no shells, and shells with no gun. It's too bad you can't combine them.'

'We tried that,' he said. 'You need a smaller barrel for the .22 cartridges.' He stopped. 'Wait a minute, where are those two empty 12-gauge shells?'

I found them. He examined their rear ends. 'Look, Lizzy. See these primers?'

I knew nothing about guns or bullets then, and little more today, but Tim showed me what he meant – a little round, dimpled piece of metal inset in the solid metal end of the shell. 'The hammer hits this primer,' he said. 'It makes a little explosion and that sets off the powder inside the shell itself.' He fumbled around for a nail and inserted it in the open end of the shell, then hit it with a piece of wood. The primer popped out and left a little hole. Tim took one of his .22 cartridges and tried to fit it into the hole, but the cartridge was too big.

'That doesn't matter,' he mumbled, reaming out the hole with the point of his knife. He worked slowly, with care, and it took a few moments, but soon he was able to slide the small .22 cartridge into the enlarged primer hole. It went almost all the way through into the empty shell, then stopped, held by the wider flange at the end of the .22 cartridge.

'Now,' he said triumphantly, 'I bet if I put this in the shotgun and fired, the .22 would go off.'

'That's wonderful,' I said, not sure whether it was or not.

Tim thought for a moment. 'But it would just rattle down that big barrel like a marble,' he said. 'It wouldn't hit the inside of a barn or knock a hole through if it did.' He took the bullet out again and examined it. Then he came to a decision and got up to work at the table. He began worrying at the slug in the front of the cartridge with his knife blade.

'Tim, be careful! What are you doing?'

'Taking out the lead.'

'Why? What are you going to do with it?'

'Melt it down, take six or seven of these little ones and make one big slug.'

'But they won't shoot, will they?'

'When I get through, they will.'

I will bypass the slow explanation he gave me, and relate to you exactly what he did, and what it resulted in. In all, his labours required the rest of the day.

First, he took out all of the tiny .22 lead slugs and put them aside. He then poured out the smokeless powder from each shell, making a pile on a small bit of paper from the Sears and Roebuck catalogue the trapper had used for all of his daily needs. This done, he reamed out a second hole in the other used shotgun shell.

'Before I go to all the rest of the work,' he said, 'I might as well see if it's going to shoot.'

He slipped one of the now empty .22 cartridges into the new hole in a used shotgun shell, put it into the breach of the shotgun, closed it, cocked the hammer, and squeezed the trigger.

The gun went 'Bang!'

It was not a loud bang – more like one from a toy cap pistol. But the sound delighted Tim. 'It works!' he yelled.

Now he asked for my help. 'Melt down one of our candles. Keep the wax hot on the stove. Be careful it doesn't catch on fire.'

'I may know nothing about firearms,' I said, 'but I have helped Miss Pauline pour candles many times. Trust me not to burn them up.'

Meanwhile he inserted two fresh .22 shells, minus their bullets and powder, into the two empty 12-gauge shotgun cylinders. I gave him the pan with the wax, and he poured a few drops into each shotgun shell very carefully.

'That'll hold the .22s in place,' he explained.

Now, as I replaced the wax on the stove, he divided the

powder he had taken from his own bullets into two heaps and, folding the paper, poured one heap into each shotgun shell.

'I need two small bits of cloth for wadding,' he said. I tore them off a rag I had been using for dishes, and he stuffed them down into the shotgun shells, using the point of his knife to tamp them.

'Wax,' he said. He poured a few more drops down on top of the wadding, then put the shells aside. 'We'll let them harden. You can clean out the pan now, and we'll use it to melt the lead.'

'Wait a minute,' I said. 'I don't know about that. Will we be able to get the extra lead out of the pan when we're through?'

'I don't know,' he said.

'Then we must find something else. We don't have pans to throw away melting lead.'

'How about a big spoon?'

I hesitated. I hated to sacrifice a spoon, but we had enough of them and it was better to lose one than a pan.

'All right,' I said.

I gave him one and he propped it on the stove. He had fourteen little slugs of lead, so he put seven of them into the spoon. To my surprise, they soon began to settle and take on a greyish appearance. Before long, they had melted into a silvery pool that almost filled the bowl of the spoon. Tim put one of the shotgun shells on the table and said : 'Go outside, Lizzy. I don't think the lead will be hot enough to melt through the wadding and set off the gunpowder, but I never did this before.'

'If you stay in this room, so do I.'

He took a double rag and held the spoon with it. He walked carefully over to the table and poured the moulten lead down into the mouth of the shotgun shell. I winced, but nothing happened.

Tim put the spoon back on the stove and added the other seven bullets. He went again and peered down into the shotgun shell.

'It's hardening,' he said. 'Those .22 slugs have turned

into one big bullet, like a minie ball.'

He followed the same procedure with the other spoonful of lead, with the same result. As soon as the shotgun shells were cool enough to handle, he gave me one. Now it was no longer an empty cardboard tube. It felt like a real shell – and deadly.

'Will they work?' I asked him.

'There's only one way to find out. But we don't have one to spare for testing. We'll have to wait until we really need to shoot them.'

'And if they don't fire?'

'We run.'

I was glad I hadn't allowed Tim to use a pan, for it proved impossible to get the excess lead out of the spoon no matter how many times I heated it and tried to wipe the moulten metal away. Eventually, I relegated the contaminated spoon to duty as stove lid lifter, which we didn't have and for which I had been using small twigs, which often broke.

The days passed. It would soon be Christmas. The thought of observing Christ's birthday away from home was repugnant to me, but there was no hope for it, so I determined to make the best of our situation. Tim had no interest in the passing dates. His eyes were fixed on the lake and its thickening ice. He kept a hole clear for us to get water from, and he tended his fish lines which occasionally produced a treat for us, and he did all the heavy chores. He rarely complained. I found myself thinking that if one must be holed up in a winter cabin, there were worse compensations than Tim Hood.

I began to store little items. Christmas dinner must be special. And I wracked my brain for a gift. We had so little, and it would do no good for me to give Tim something that I would only need to borrow back.

Meanwhile he took the shotgun and his two cartridges and roamed far from the cabin, searching for the bear.

'He'll come back when he's hungry again,' Tim insisted. 'I'd rather shoot him in the outdoors. Then if he's only wounded, he'll crawl off somewhere. If I wounded him inside the cabin, he might turn on us.'

'But why kill him at all?'

Sternly Tim said: 'He's already attacked this cabin twice. Next time he might catch one of us – or ruin the cabin, which would be about the same thing. Lizzy, we've *got* to kill him. Don't you see?'

'Yes. But I'm still sorry for him.'

One day Tim caught a particularly large pike. He brought it to me and said: 'Lizzy, can we get by without eating this one?'

I had been smiling at its obvious fat and was taken by surprise. 'Why?'

'I want to use it to bait the bear.'

'How will you do that?'

'We'll partially cook the fish to let the scent out. Then I'll take a piece of cloth and tie it up on the side of a tree away from the cabin, where we can watch it. If the bear is nearby, he'll smell the fish and come to investigate. Then maybe I can get a shot.'

I was tired of hearing about the bear, so I said, 'Oh, all right. But see that you catch another fish to replace this one.'

That night, his preparations complete, Tim took the fish out and hung it from the limb of a nearby birch. 'That ought to fetch him,' he said, satisfied.

It didn't, though. We watched that dead fish for three days before we gave up in disgust and forgot about it.

Tim put the shotgun in the shed. I would not have it in the house now that it was loaded.

The weather deepened. True winter was upon us, and there was no break to its chill. My father's prediction of a winterkill seemed to be coming true when we came on a small deer hardly more than a fawn, frozen in a snow drift. We didn't dare take it for food because we couldn't be sure it hadn't died of disease. It was an unhappy foreboding of what was to come.

Each morning the ice on the lake was thicker, until one

day our water hole was completely frozen over too thick to break through.

'I will have to go out where the ice is thinner,' Tim said.

It is good that I stayed there, fearful, because Tim had gone no more than ten steps from shore when he broke through. He yelled and began to thrash about. I was afraid he would sink under the ice, and shouted, 'Don't move! I'll pull you out.'

I found a long stick and inched my way out on to the ice. It swayed and trembled under my feet. It took all my courage to get close enough to Tim to reach him with the stick. He caught it frantically, and my feet went out from under me. I was being drawn towards the dark water.

'Wait!' I screamed. I dug my heels in and somehow found a grip. Then he crawled up on to the ice, coughing and groaning. The air was so cold that the water was already freezing in his hair and on his clothes. I hurried him up to the cabin and made him undress all the way down to his skin.

When he protested modestly, I yelled: 'Have some sense or you will die of pneumonia!' I threw a dry blanket around him and hung his clothes up to dry. Meanwhile he sipped a cup of spruce tea and for once didn't complain that he didn't like it.

While he was getting warm I went out and with the long stick retrieved the bucket which hadn't gone into the water.

When I came back, Tim had put on his other jeans and was huddled near the stove. 'I'm sorry,' he said.

'Be glad I was there.'

'I am. You're always there. You're the best sister a fellow ever had.'

'Thank you.'

Later that evening, he went out and came back with a bucket of water. I didn't ask how he had got it without falling in again. He went to bed right after supper, saying that he felt very tired. But after I turned the lamp out, I could hear him turning restlessly.

The bear came early the next morning. I looked out the window and there he was, standing up on his hind legs, clawing at the fish hung in the birch trees.

'Tim!' I hissed.

'The gun is in the shed!' he said. 'You stay here. Lock the door after me. But open it fast if he chases me.'

Trembling I latched the door and hurried back to the window. The bear didn't know we were there. He was only interested in the smelly fish hung up just out of his reach. He was very black and looked moth-eaten. I had seen bears before, so I wasn't surprised at how much like a man he looked. But the snorts and grunts he made were new. I had never heard a bear 'speak' before.

Tim crept towards the baited tree, staying low in the snow. The bear must have smelled him, for he stopped clawing at the fish, stood on his hind feet, and looked around. Tim raised the shotgun. The bear turned towards him.

'Shoot, Tim!' I screamed.

Tim waited until the bear took a step away from the tree. Then I saw the muzzle of the old shotgun jump up in the air, belching smoke, and there came a terrible explosion of sound. I saw black fur fly from the bear's middle, and he lurched back with a yelp.

Tim left the shotgun in the snow and ran for the cabin. I had the door open when he got there. We slammed it and locked it and rushed back to the window. The bear was down on all fours, running in circles, biting at his stomach.

'It worked!' Tim said. 'We got him.'

'Duck!' I said. The bear had stood up and was looking at us. We stayed down until our nerves could stand it no longer, then took a quick peek. The bear was no longer there.

'He's gone,' I said.

'Maybe he's coming for the cabin,' Tim said. 'Why didn't I keep the gun?'

I ran to the other window. There was nothing in sight but blowing snow.

'No,' I said. 'I guess he ran back in the woods.'

We waited for half an hour, then Tim slipped outside carefully. I saw him pick up the shotgun and reload it, then move cautiously towards the birch tree. There he bent over and examined the ground. He looked out into the forest.

When he came inside again, he said: 'I think he's hurt bad. He bled all over, and there were black lumps in it.'

'What should we do?'

'I want some breakfast,' Tim said. 'We'll give the bear an hour or so to die, then I'm going in to look for him.'

'Oh no you're not!'

'I had to shoot him. But he's also food, the best kind we can get. You remember what Dad said.'

'But he could hurt you.'

'I have one shell left. Boy, I mean to tell you, that old shotgun kicked like a mule. Did you see the way he went down? It must have been like getting shot with a thirty-aught-six. I'd bet you a nickel he's dead right now.'

'I'll come with you,' I said.

'No, you stay here. If he's only wounded, I can outrun him, but not with you along.'

'I can run faster than you can.'

'Not since you hurt your ankle. Now don't argue, Lizzy.'

I fed him, and we waited by the fire. I knew from the way Tim acted that he was none too keen to set off on the trail of the bear, but he took his duty like a soldier and after an hour or so had gone by, stood up.

'Now, don't you worry if I'm gone awhile,' he said. 'I aim to move slow and double back and forth across his trail so he can't lay for me.'

The thought of the bear lurking in ambush sent chills up my back. Again, I pleaded with Tim not to go. 'We don't need the food,' I said. 'We have plenty.'

'It may be another month until the ice is thick enough to cross,' he said. 'I'd feel better knowing we wouldn't have to leave here just because we were hungry.'

So reluctantly I let him out-argue me. He was right. Our supplies were getting skimpy. We had been eating too many precious potatoes, and the onions had dwindled down to about a dozen. We would have much to answer for when the trapper returned — if he ever did — which I had begun to doubt.

I gave Tim some food to carry and made sure he had matches and his knife.

'Please be careful, Timmy,' I said.

'Have plenty of spruce tea ready,' he laughed, and left. I watched him from the window. He seemed so small and frail under the heavy shotgun. He didn't look back or wave.

Never have hours crawled so slowly. It was just as well that we didn't have a clock. Its ticking would have driven me mad. As it was, I wore a path to the window and kept the cabin chilled with my constant forays outside. I busied myself in every way I could find. I found the new hole near the shore that Tim had broken open for fresh water and carried some to refill the pots. When that was done, I cut wood with the saw for an hour until I was so cold my fingers wouldn't close over its handle.

How could I have let him go out into the woods alone? True, I wouldn't be able to run so well with my weak ankle, but —

Such recriminations were stupid, and I stopped them. Instead, I prayed.

Night came, but Tim did not.

By morning I was frantic. I couldn't sleep, although I dozed by the fire which I kept going. I put the lamp in the window facing the direction Tim had gone so he would be able to see it if he should come out of the woods by some miracle during the night. But it was wasted kerosene.

When it was light enough, I dressed myself warmly and, taking the largest kitchen knife, set off following Tim's tracks. They were easy to follow, since they were in deep snow for the first few hundred yards. But once I got inside the trees, the going was harder. Often I lost them entirely and only picked them up again by searching back and forth, using as a centre line the occasional drops of blood left by the bear.

During the first hour, I called his name often but got no answer. I couldn't tell how far I had gone, since the walking was difficult, and I wasted a lot of time picking up the trail. Here, deep under the trees, the snow was often hard and crusty and did not hold tracks at all.

Sometime in the morning, I stopped. I lifted my head and sniffed. I smelled wood smoke – there was no mistaking it – and mixed with the smoke, something else: the aroma of roasted meat.

I hurried over a little knoll and came upon Tim seated comfortably on a fallen tree, roasting a huge chunk of meat over a camp fire.

'Tim!' I rushed towards him and fell down in the snow. I got up and fell again.

'Don't break your neck. What are you doing here?'

Struggling towards him, I gasped: 'You had me worried sick. Where have you been?'

'That old bear went farther than I thought. By the time I found him, it was getting dark. He was dead, so I dressed him out and made a camp there under some limbs. I brushed away the snow right down to the ground, and put some spruce boughs there. It was warmer than you'd think.'

'Well, why didn't you come right back this morning?'

He indicated a large fur-covered bundle beside him. 'I started to. See? That's a front leg. I got this far and was awfully hungry. So I made a fire, and that's what I intend to do as soon as this chunk is cooked.'

I yelled at him for worrying me, but I was so glad to see him that it lacked conviction. In a few minutes, the meat was ready to eat. We gobbled it down without salt or anything. It was greasy and good.

'As long as you're here,' Tim said, 'we might as well go back and drag some more of the bear this way.'

He led me through the woods. The going was easier,

137

with him breaking trail. We must have walked for an hour. Then we came upon the carcass of the bear sprawled in a little hollow.

'Hey!' yelled Tim. 'Shoo!'

Something small and brown ran away from the bear and scurried over a snowbank.

'What was that?' I asked.

'Fox. He's been having breakfast on our bear.'

'Ugh.'

The fox had crawled inside the bear's body cavity to eat part of the liver. I criticized Tim for not having taken it out first. 'There's more food value in the liver than any other part of the meat,' I said.

Calmly he replied: 'Yes, but I don't particularly like liver.'

Tim was growing up before my eyes.

'Well,' I compromised, 'we'll take it now, if it is all right with you.'

He agreed, and cut it away from the cavity. It was a big double handful, dark red, almost purple. It steamed slightly in the freezing air.

'He's still a little warm,' Tim said.

We put the liver aside and began to try and sever the hindquarters. It was hard going with only a knife.

'We need a saw,' Tim grunted, cutting away.

'That would take all day to fetch,' I said. 'Maybe we can cut the bear straight across the belly.'

We tried there. It was easy enough to slice between the ribs, but when we came to the heavy backbone, the knife was stopped cold. Tim worried at it for half an hour but couldn't make a dent. He stopped when he chipped a nick out of his knife.

'It's no use, Lizzy,' he said. 'We have to saw those big bones.'

I looked around. I saw the pile of stones he had used for his camp fire. 'Wait,' I said. 'Let's try something else.'

We propped two of the large stones directly under the bear's back. 'All right,' I said, taking up another rock, 'let's see if we can make this do.'

Tim smashed at the backbone with the rock. It made wet, meaty sounds against the flesh. 'I don't know,' he said after a while. 'I think maybe it gave a little.'

'Jump on it,' I said.

He did, and the bone splintered.

It was then only a matter of minutes to cut carefully through the spine and separate the hindquarters and lower back from the rest of the bear.

But dragging it through the woods was another matter. We each took a foot and, with the liver fastened to the top by some string, set off. The bear's hair matted in the snow, and held us back, and the going was difficult. We would pull for twenty steps and then stop and rest. It took us the rest of the day to get back to the cabin. We were both prostrate with exhaustion. We threw ourselves down on the beds gasping before we were able to find the energy to start a fire in the stove.

'The shotgun is still out there with that front leg,' Tim said.

'No one will steal it,' I said.

We left the bear's hindquarters out in the snow where they had been abandoned when we staggered into the cabin. Nothing would eat on them this close to the cabin, and if they did, they were welcome to what they could get.

Tim was up early. He set out for the front leg and the shotgun while I made breakfast and was back in a little over an hour. We had hot coffee and bear liver fried with onions. Delicious. The liver was stronger than venison but still tasty.

'This time,' Tim said, 'we take the saw.'

We did, and it made sawing the remainder of the bear into two chunks, minus the head, easy. We had them both back to the cabin by nightfall. While I made supper, Tim began skinning out the carcass before hanging it in the shed.

Bedtime came none too soon. It had been a tiring two days, but now we had plenty of fat meat to see us through the next few weeks. More than that, we didn't have to fear the bear rampaging our cabin again.

As we lay in the darkness, Tim said: 'Do you think the kids at school will believe us when we tell them about this?'

'No,' I said. 'It would be better to keep it to ourselves or they'll brand us as terrible liars.'

He laughed. 'I'd call us liars myself, if I weren't here to see it.'

'You heard what my father said before. It is a hard thing to starve to death in the woods if only you keep your head.'

Tim didn't answer for a while, then said: 'Yes, I remember him saying that.'

I had hurt him again and was sorry. 'Would you like to hear a story?'

'No,' he said. 'Good night, Lizzy.'

'Good night, Timmy,' I said.

We had a tree for Christmas, a spindly little hemlock with a bushy top. Tim cut it and made a rude stand to keep it standing. We put it in the corner of the room. I decorated it with pine cones which I had been gathering, hanging them like Christmas balls from the branches. I dangled our extra silverware from the lower boughs and shaped a star from some tinfoil which had been in an old empty tobacco package I found in the trash box. We put the tree up on Christmas eve after supper. When it was finished, we sat near the stove and sang Christmas songs. I was happier than I had been since the canoe turned over. I had two wonderful surprises for Tim and couldn't wait to spring them on him.

But they would have to wait until morning. Meanwhile I recited all of 'The Night Before Christmas.' Though he scoffed that it was a poem for little kids, I could tell he was pleased.

'I wish we were home,' Tim said softly.

'So do I. But wait until next year! We'll have a great big tree, all covered with candy canes and popcorn balls, and coloured decorations and we'll have a roast turkey with stuffing, and pumpkin pie and — '

'Stop it, Lizzy,' he said, his voice muffled. He had turned away from me. I had upset him by reminding him of home.

I was tempted to tell him of his present then, but I didn't want to spoil his surprise. So I said, 'I'm sorry, Tim. I'll make a nice Christmas dinner for you tomorrow.'

'I know you will,' he said, his voice trembling.

As I tell our story now, relating the difficulties we encountered and the hazards we overcame, it is so easy to think of Tim and myself as we later became — adults — for all memory is coloured by what has gone between. But for all our adventures, we were only children. So it isn't so hard to understand that we would give in to childish fears and despair every now and then. I'm surprised that we endured as well as we did.

Despite our singing and efforts to remain cheerful, the fact that it was Christmas eve only served to remind us that we were alone and lost deep in the woods far from home.

We went to bed early. Although I tried not to listen, I heard Tim whisper his prayers. Neither of us had been very good about nightly prayers under the best of conditions, and I had just about forsaken them after my father died. But now I let the words tumble from my lips. Along with Tim, I whispered : '. . . if I should die before I wake, I pray the Lord my soul to take.'

'Amen,' I said out loud.

'Amen,' Tim repeated.

'What's this?' Tim cried, peering under the tree. We had slept late, and I let him get up first to start the fire, because Christmas or not, it was his turn. I sat up and looked where he was pointing.

There was a small package, wrapped in a page from the Sears and Roebuck catalogue, nestled under the balsam.

Tim picked it up. 'It's got my name written on it,' he said.

He held it up and shook it. 'What is it?'

'Well, there's one sure way to find out.'

'Should I open it?'

'No, stupid! Plant it, and maybe it'll come up in the spring and grow a dozen.'

He untied the string carefully. We saved everything to use again. Slowly he unwrapped the paper. He stared at it.

'Oh, Lizzy! Mittens! Thank you.'

It hadn't been easy, for I didn't have much time when he was not watching. Whenever Tim had been in the woods, I had worked on his present. I unravelled part of one of the extra blankets for the wool. Although I didn't have a regular set of crocheting needles, I had driven four nails into the end of a piece of wood and had used it much as we used to crochet with a thread spool at home. I poked the strands of wool through the nails with a single needle I had carved from a long twig. Nor did I try to make the mittens in one piece. I laid out a pattern for the right hand and one for the left, and then made two of each, and lock-stitched them together. The result was a pair of the drabest, ugliest, ill-fittingest mittens I had ever seen. But they were warm, and poor Tim spent so much time out in the cold that they would comfort him.

He hugged me. 'How did you do it? When did you have time?'

'Santa Claus and his elves helped,' I said. 'Now, I must get to work on dinner. There's cold meat from last night. Take some and go out on your trap line. Don't come back for at least three hours, because I don't want to be disturbed.'

'All right,' he said. 'I have to move some of the traps anyway. I found some new runways that look good.'

'Be careful and don't get too far from the cabin. The sky looks like snow.'

'I won't,' he said. Then at the door: 'Lizzy?'

'Yes?'

'Merry Christmas.'

'Merry Christmas, Tim.'

As soon as he had gone, I went to work. I had hidden

supplies all over the cabin. My biggest problem had been to find a substitute for flour. The escaped convict had taken what little had been in the cabin. It was possible to grind up certain nuts and roots for flour, but I had neither. But I had heard of potato pancakes. Was it possible to make flour from potatoes? I had decided to try, and had roasted and dried several and then pulverized their pulp. I dried that again several times and had to admit that it *looked* like flour. The question was, would it behave like flour?

Well, there was no better time to find out. I added water to the powdered potatoes and blended in some dried yeast and margarine, then kneaded the mass into a ball and put it near the fire. As I went about my other chores, I kept glancing at the 'dough' and after an hour or so noted, to my delight, that it was rising.

Unknown to Tim, I had hoarded a large partridge. The birds were scarce now, and I had kept this one hidden behind a box in the supply shed. I put it near the stove to thaw while I divided the potato dough into two parts. One half I put aside; the other I rolled out and draped over one of our tin plates which I put on top of the stove to bake, covering it with a pot to form a homemade oven. Then I cut up an onion and mixed it into the other half of the dough, which I flavoured with salt and pepper and put aside. This would be dressing for the bird.

The partridge was thawed enough to pluck now, which I did. Then I painted it liberally with margarine and put it into the large pot and poured just enough water in the bottom to keep it from burning. I covered it and put it on to bake.

For vegetables, I boiled a mixture of diced onions, potatoes, and some of the last of the wild greens.

The pie crust was done now, and I took it off the stove. I opened the can of peaches I had been saving from the last of the trapper's stores and poured them into the pie shell. A moment or two on the stove while we ate the main course, and Tim would have his favourite pie – peach cobbler.

Once the partridge was partially browned, I spooned in

the dressing mixture and put it back on the stove. I kept the fire low so as not to burn the bird, and the cabin was cool as a result. Now that the snow was piled high up against its sides, we didn't have much trouble keeping it warm. But we still kept one of the cabin windows ajar, remembering our mishap earlier in the winter.

I wished for some flavouring with which I could make a good drink, but there was nothing but coffee or spruce needles. I decided on coffee, which I weakened with condensed milk.

While the bird continued to cook, I set the table. And none too soon, either, for no sooner was I done than I heard Tim stamping his feet outside. He entered, accompanied by a cold draft.

'It's starting to snow,' he said. 'There are animals out all over the woods, feeding. That's a sure sign we're in for a bad storm.'

'Well, we are snug as two bugs in here,' I said. 'Let it storm. Take off your coat. Dinner is ready.'

'Smells good,' he said, wrinkling his nose. 'Is that bear meat?'

'I will slap your face, Timothy Hood!' I said. 'Wash your hands.'

As he did, he said, 'We got one rabbit; that's all. But I put one of the big traps in the middle of a deer runway and tied it to a tree. If a small enough deer comes along, we just might give him a surprise.'

'I have a surprise for you,' I said. 'Sit down at the table.'

His eyes popped as I served the baked partridge. 'You carve,' I said, 'while I get the vegetables.'

He cut us each a drumstick. 'What is this?' he said. 'Dressing?'

'Nothing else.'

'You are a bob-tailed wonder,' he said. 'I thought that jailbird took all our flour.'

'I have one or two tricks up my sleeves,' I said, smiling.

I had put the pie on to bake. As we ate, its aroma filled the room. Tim sniffed.

'I am surely going crazy,' he said. 'I could swear that I smell peach cobbler.'

'Maybe Santa Claus has been busy again.'

'If there's peach cobbler, I think I have to agree with you.'

'Well, prepare to thank Old Saint Nick,' I said, getting up. I took the pie over to the window shelf to slice. As I looked out, I saw that it was now snowing quite hard. It was almost as dark as night outside.

The pie could have used some nutmeg, but it was still good. You could hardly tell the potato flour from regular pie crust. It was too bad we didn't have more potatoes in the shed. But our supply was too low to let us waste it on any more pie crusts. In fact, I was concerned about our dwindling supplies and the increasing snow. There was still food to be gathered during the winter, but deep snow would make it difficult.

'Is the ice any thicker?' I asked Tim.

'Some. But there is still plenty of open water out on the lake.' He finished his pie. 'Thinking about that trail?'

'I wish we didn't have to wait another month.'

'But it was you who said it's still too dangerous.'

'I know. That doesn't prevent me from wishing.'

We drank some of the diluted coffee. Then Tim said: 'I know it's not my turn, but I'm going to do the dishes.'

'You will have to get some water, then. I used it all cooking.'

He slipped into his coat. 'You sit by the fire. The rest of the chores are mine.' He looked down at his hands. 'I'm sorry I didn't have a present for you. I'm ashamed.'

'Go on,' I said. 'You're a boy. Were you supposed to knit me a cap!'

'No, but I should have thought of something.'

'Doing today's chores is present enough. But get on with them before the snow fills up your water hole.'

'I'm on my way,' he said, starting to the door. But he never reached it. It opened suddenly, and in stepped the escaped convict.

*

When he had eaten everything in sight, the man wiped his mouth and belched.

'You are a pig,' I said.

'Shut your mouth, little girl,' he said. 'Or I'll darned well shut it for you.'

'What do you want this time?' Tim demanded.

The man smiled, but it was not a pleasant smile. 'I see your father and uncle never got back.'

'What business is that of yours?' I said. 'The truth is, when we told them what you had done, they went out to report it to the sheriff and bring back a posse.'

'Is that so?' said the convict. He picked his teeth with the blade of his knife. 'Well, little lady, I hate to be the bearer of bad tidings. You see, I found your father's boat, what was left of it, floating upside down in the lake. So I suppose you'd better not wait any longer for him.'

'We'll wait if we want to,' I said, my lip trembling. For what he said was close to the bone. I was lying to him about the trapper, but my own father lay dead up-river, and that was what brought the tears to my eyes.

'Then you'll be waiting for a ghost,' said the convict. He turned to Tim and snapped: 'What's your name?'

Startled, Tim gave it.

'And yours?'

He was speaking to me. 'I am Elizabeth,' I said stiffly.

'Then I will call you Betty,' he said.

Knowing it was foolish, but so angry that I could not stop myself, I cried, 'You will call me nothing at all, Mr Escaped Convict.'

His eyes widened. 'Oh? Where do you get that idea?'

'I heard all about you on the radio.'

He looked around. 'There's no radio here.'

'That was before we packed in.'

He thought about that. 'Okay,' he said. 'Now that we know who you are, I'll tell you about me. You can call me Mr Sharp.'

'More likely, your name is Dull,' I said.

'You have a snippy tongue, Missy,' he said. 'I know how to cure that – if you force me to it. You're right.

Sharp ain't my real name, but it's the one the law calls me by — and that's good enough for you.'

'Then you *are* a convict!' said Tim.

Sharp whirled around. 'What do you know?' he demanded. 'I ain't a thief. Yes, I escaped. But I never wore chains, and I never will, not in this world.'

'If you're not a convict, why were you in jail?' Tim said.

Smiling tightly, Sharp said: 'I killed a man.'

I backed away from him. He turned to me. 'Does that scare you, Sweet Thing? You don't mind if I call you Sweet Thing, do you?'

'I mind if you call me anything,' I said. 'I don't enjoy the sound of your voice. Why are you here? If you're escaping, you ought to be on your way out of the state.'

'In good time,' Sharp said. 'I don't intend to be gathered up again and sent to that little room down at Sing Sing with its big electric chair. I'm sure all those who broke out with me have already been recaptured. But I'm too smart for the law. I headed for the woods because that's the last place they'll look for me.'

'And now you are caught in the woods and can't get out without being spotted,' I said.

'You are very sharp, Sweet Thing,' he told me.

'You stop calling her that,' said Tim.

Sharp belted him across the chest with his huge paw of a hand and Tim fell against the table, knocking off one of the plates which broke on the floor.

I snatched up the butcher knife. 'Don't hit him again,' I said, 'or you'll have me to answer to.'

Sharp fell back against the wall, laughing. 'You're some baby, Sweet Thing,' he said. 'I like your spunk.'

Tim got up. 'Put the knife away, Lizzy,' he said. 'This man is the kind of coward who hits children and shoots men in the back.'

'What do you want here?' I asked. 'You stole all of our supplies on your last visit. There's nothing left for you to take.'

'Oh,' he said, shaking his finger, 'you two played a good

one on me then. I got out of here fast because I didn't want to meet up with the rest of your family. But now that we all know they're at the bottom of the lake, I can afford to take my time. And if you had no supplies left, what have you been living on? Where did that partridge come from? If you had no flour, how did you bake a peach pie?'

'I made that from potatoes,' I said – and then clapped my hand over my mouth.

'Ah, 'said Sharp. 'And where did you find potatoes?'

'I shall not lie to you,' I said. 'For you would only find me out. But I won't help you, either. You'll steal us blind and then leave us here to die.'

'You're very wrong, Sweet Thing,' Sharp said. 'The last thing I want is for you to die. You're going to be a big help to me.'

'I wouldn't help you with water if you were perishing on the flaming desert,' I told him.

'Tim,' he said, 'run and get me some potatoes.'

'No,' Tim said. Sharp raised his hand again, and Tim faced up to it squarely. 'If you strike me again,' he said, 'I'll kill you.'

Sharp laughed and said: 'How will you arrange that? Where's your weapon? I'm bigger and stronger.'

'I'll find a way,' Tim promised.

Sharp said: 'I'm still hungry. I want a dish of fried potatoes. Get them for me, and then we'll be friends.'

Tim looked at me. I didn't want to help this loathsome man, but neither did I want Tim to be struck again. I knew Sharp wasn't bluffing. 'Go and get his potatoes,' I said.

As Tim left, Sharp said: 'You two are both blood-thirsty little monsters, ain't you? I thought I had seen hard cases inside the walls, but they don't hold a candle to the both of you.'

'If you'd been on your own in this wilderness for the better part of three months, scratching a living out of the snow, you might be a hard case too,' I said. If I had thought to soften his heart, it was a false hope, for he only threw back his head and laughed. 'We'll get along, Sweet Thing, you and I. We're both tough as shoe leather. How old are you?'

'That is none of your concern,' I said.

'Seventeen? Eighteen?' I stared at him, but he didn't seem to be joking. I decided to let him think what he wished, for it might turn out to be helpful. 'You couldn't be older than twenty,' he said.

'I'm small for my age,' I said and let him chew on that.

Tim returned with several potatoes. Sharp snatched one, rubbed it on his sleeve, and began to eat it raw.

'If you hold off, I'll cook them for you,' I said. 'I wouldn't ask even an escaped convict to eat raw potatoes.'

'Then get to work instead of talking about it,' he said. 'Tim, where did you get these? They're cold, but they're not frozen. Come on, answer me and be quick about it or you'll get yours.'

'We have a shed behind the cabin,' I said.

Sharp nodded, grinning. 'And it's filled with potatoes and other good things?'

'I wish it was. Our provisions are very short, and you're not helping matters with your gluttony.'

'A lot you know, Missy,' he shot back. 'I would like to see you out in the woods, cold and wet and nothing to eat in sight.'

'We've been there,' I said. 'And we weren't cold, wet, or hungry. If you had taken the trouble to learn about the woods before you decided to move into them, you'd have nothing to complain about.'

'Cook those potatoes,' he ordered, then added: 'So you kids know your way around these woods?'

Before I could stop him, Tim said, 'Well enough to get you turned around in circles!'

'Then I'll take care not to trust you,' Sharp replied.

'How did you find this lake?' I asked.

'I followed the trail,' he said. 'There was a boat up on the shore, turned upside down, so I launched it and crossed the lake.'

'Directly across?' I asked, trying to keep the question casual.

'Until I spotted this inlet and this cabin.' My heart soared. That meant there was a landing and a trail once we cleared the point. He went on. 'I suppose the boat belonged to your father?'

'No,' I said. 'Our landing is over to the right. You must have stolen the game warden's boat. He's probably looking for it.'

'When will you stop trying to gaff me, Sweet Thing? Nobody's looking for me. Not for you neither or they would have been here by now. You're trying to tie me in circles for your own good.'

Sullenly Tim said, 'If you're going to steal our supplies, take them and go.'

'You don't mind if I wait until the snowstorm is over, do you?'

We didn't answer. I put the potatoes on to fry. Sharp watched with alert, hungry eyes. When they were done, he ate them down, every one, without offering any to us. He patted his stomach and sighed: 'I've gotten very tired of boiled beans.'

'That was your own fault,' I said. 'There's plenty to eat in the woods if you'll work for it.'

He was more cheerful now. Picking his teeth, he said: 'You're just like two little wild animals, do you know that? I wouldn't want to meet up with you after dark. Where do you come from?'

'That is for us to know and you to find out,' I told him.

He scowled. 'What's the point in acting like that? I was only trying to be friendly.'

'I'd as soon be friendly with a polecat,' I said. 'At least, a polecat will show you his stripes and let you know what kind of animal he is. But you walk like a man and behave like a snake.'

'All right,' he said. 'That's more than enough. As soon as this snowstorm is over, we'll pack the boat and be on our way.'

'What do you mean, *we*? We're not going with you.'

'That's all you know,' he said. 'You're my ticket out of these woods. They're looking for a man alone. They wouldn't even question a father and his two children. You can keep the law off my back.'

'You're soft in the head,' I said. 'We have no intention of helping you.'

'You'll help me – or else. Don't give me any more argument. Don't even open your mouth, Missy. Do your chores and shut up. One kid will do as good as two, if it comes to that.'

It grew dark, and the snow still fell. Sharp yawned. 'It'll be nice to bunk down in a soft bed,' he said. 'Whose will I take? Yours, Tim? Or Sweet Thing's?'

'Take either one you wish,' I said. 'We'll make do.'

'Yes, I'm sure you will,' he said with a wink. I turned away, sick inside.

Before he turned in, he showed us my father's .44 revolver. It was rusted all over now. Sharp had taken no care of it at all; I hated him for that.

'Don't get any ideas,' he said. 'I have this, and I'm a very light sleeper. So don't rattle any knives or pick up any heavy chairs. Like I said, I don't need both of you to help me with the law. One will do. I wouldn't mind leaving the other one here.'

'We never disturb sleeping dogs,' I said.

'Aw!' he growled. 'You're enough to make an angel swear.'

'What would you know of angels?'

Tim touched my arm and shook his head. We finished cleaning up and sat on Tim's bed, whispering. Sharp seemed to be asleep, but I couldn't be sure.

'I don't think we should make him angry,' Tim said.

'But he's a terrible man and a murderer, too.'

'Yes, but he can take us out of here.'

'And then what? Do you think he'll release us in the middle of town to give the alarm? I don't think so. I think once he has no more use for us, he'll take care of us in some permanent way.'

'But what else can we do?'

151

'I'm not sure,' I said. 'Go to sleep, Tim. We can't do anything tonight. I'll think about it.'

'You take the bed,' he said. 'I can sleep on the floor.' I argued, but he insisted.

I didn't blow out the lamp but merely turned it down until the room barely glowed in its light. I didn't relish being in a dark room with a man like Sharp.

There wasn't the slightest doubt in my mind that he meant us harm. We would be allowed to serve his purposes until he no longer needed us. Then he would cut our throats with no more qualm than a butcher sticking a pig. Somehow we had to get away from him. But Tim had a point. Better to let him get us out of the woods and then escape – if we could. We could run back in the woods and hide, but that would mean almost certain death, for he would probably burn the cabin out of meanness and we would have no supplies, no tools, no hope.

While pondering these problems, I fell asleep.

My father woke me. I felt his hand touch my shoulder.

'Father,' I said. 'I had the most awful dream. I dreamed we were lost in the big woods, and the snow was everywhere, and we were alone in a trapper's cabin on a lake. I dreamed that the canoe turned over, and that you were . . .' I couldn't say it and began to sniffle.

Something tightened about my throat. I tried to scream but couldn't make a sound.

A voice said: 'I don't need both of you, and you're the one who'll cause trouble.'

This was not my father! I twisted out of the grasp. I was back in the trapper's cabin and Sharp was crouched over me. I threw my head back and screamed.

'Shut up!' he snarled and struck me. My ears rang, and I saw stars. I fell back, and his hands clawed at me. I began to cry. 'Damn it,' he said, 'you were just asking for it! You're nothing but bad news!'

I couldn't speak. All I could do was scream, and every time I did, he hit me again. I felt blood running down inside my throat, and my nose was numb. Then the blows ceased. Sharp yelled and crumpled over me, and I saw Tim standing there, a broken chair in his hands. He lifted it again, and brought it down on Sharp's shoulder. The convict yelled, and reached under his pillow.

He came out with the pistol. I threw myself at him and caught his hand with both of mine, but I wasn't strong enough. I lowered my head and bit his wrist with all my might. He hit me with his other hand and knocked me off the bed.

'Run, Tim!' I shrieked.

But Tim was already on the move. He darted out the door. Sharp fired the pistol. It made a bright orange flame in the darkened room. The explosion deafened me. I saw bark fly from one of the logs near the door.

'Little bastard!' Sharp mumbled, heading for the door. I grabbed at his leg, but he kicked me away and my head struck the foot of the bed. I suppose I must have been unconscious for a while, for everything else is hazy in my memory. I recall hearing shouting, which was Sharp calling for Tim to reveal himself. Then – how much later I do not know – there was a dull, muffled shot, and that is when I came back to my senses. I was dizzy when I stood up. I had to hold the edge of the door, but I peered out into the snow-filled darkness and yelled: 'Tim? Tim? Are you hurt?'

There was no answer. I knew, with a sickening certainty, that evil man had shot Tim dead and was even now dragging his body to the edge of the lake to throw it in. I looked wildly around the room for a weapon. All I could find was the butcher knife. I took it and hid myself behind the door. When Sharp returned, I resolved to throw myself on him and if I could not kill him, I would sell my life dearly.

After waiting for what seemed an hour, I heard footsteps crunching in the snow. I stiffened. When they came near the door, I made a lunge, stabbing blindly with the knife.

'Lizzy!' It was Tim's voice.

It was Tim who stood in the open door. Not Sharp. Tim!

I threw myself into his arms and sobbed, 'Oh, Tim! What happened? I thought he had shot you.'

He showed me the rusty .44 revolver. 'No,' he said. 'He slipped in the snow and dropped this. I grabbed it and fired a shot in the air and he ran away. He will not be back. He is a coward. Now that we have this gun, he'll run.'

I slammed the door and bolted it. 'He is also a sneak,' I said. 'He might try to creep up during the night.'

'Not tonight,' Tim said. 'And we'll be leaving tomorrow.'

'But how?' I stared at him. Was this little Tim, always asking me what to do next, crying when his feelings were hurt? 'The ice isn't solid yet.'

'Sharp will lend us his boat,' Tim said. 'I shouted after him that I would keep guard over it tonight. He doesn't dare test me. I promised to shoot him if I saw one hair. We can take it tomorrow and row across the lake.'

But I was still worried about Sharp getting back to the cabin. Finally, Tim said that he would stand guard for the rest of the night while I slept. Then he would sleep while I made breakfast and began packing. So I stretched myself out on Tim's bed (I couldn't bear to lie in the one the convict had used) and tried to sleep.

The wind howled across the lake, and water chopped against the side of the boat, sloshing in. Tim rowed steadily while I bailed. We had brought only two blankets, some food, matches, and our knives. We knew that the trail would be choked with snow and that we had to travel light.

I suppose I must have slept during those last dark hours of the morning, for suddenly it was daylight. Instead of keeping his promise to sleep, Tim went out to the shed and loaded some small pieces of meat into the boat. I offered to help, but he refused, so sternly that I was afraid to pursue the subject. This was not like Tim.

154

The boat was half full of snow, but we scooped it out. It wasn't much of a boat. Like most of the rowboats of that day, it was made of wood, and now it was rotten wood. The oarlocks were loose and squeaked. The oars didn't match and were almost impossible to stroke. But despite all, we made slow progress. The cabin receded behind our stern.

Just as we were casting off, Tim had clapped his hand to his head and said: 'Oh, I forgot something.'

Eager to help, for he had done most of the work, I said: 'What is it? I'll go.'

'I left my knife in the shed.'

I jumped out of the boat. He shouted: 'You get back in the boat, Elizabeth Allison!'

I did. 'What's eating you, Tim?'

'Nothing. I'll be right back.'

He took five minutes to find his knife. Then when he returned, he was in one almighty hurry. We were underway in seconds after his feet touched the boat's bottom.

We were just rounding the point, where the wind caught us, when I noticed the smoke.

'Tim!' I shouted. 'Look at the cabin.'

Plumes of white smoke were spiralling up over the trees. They spewed out in great gusts. Then I saw an orange tongue of flame which seemed to come from the supply shed.

'It's on fire!' I yelled over the howl of the wind.

'The lamp must have fallen over,' Tim said, giving the cabin only the shortest glance. 'Too bad. But there's nothing we can do.' He kept rowing.

'Maybe Sharp set fire to it, thinking we were inside,' I said.

Tim didn't answer. His mouth was set, and although it was below freezing on the lake, he had sweat on his forehead.

We found the landing and made our way out along the trail. It took four days and three nights. Every night was a nightmare, as the wind shook the trees and snow fell in heavy lumps, breaking free from the branches. Once Tim got a whole load down his neck. This time, instead of laughing, I hurried to help him get it out, for the time of laughter was over. We couldn't afford to lose time or to get wet. If we had thought the winter was bad until now, it was showing its teeth and proving how terrible it really could be. I admit that I would have lain down in the snow and refused to go any further, perishing there, if it hadn't been for Tim.

'I was right,' he taunted. 'You're a quitter, Miss Lizzy. You're very high and mighty when things are going your way, but let them get tough and you lay down.'

'You'll get yours when we're home,' I promised him grimly, slogging one foot in front of the other. Each camp fire was an effort. Wood was scarce, buried under two feet of snow. We lost the trail often and had to find it again by beating our way back and forth or even retracing our steps to find where we had gone wrong. But each day brought us farther down the mountain, and my instinct told me that was the proper direction.

The last night, we camped in a clump of pines. Before a meagre fire, we huddled in our blankets and talked.

'I do not know what'll happen if we don't find a road in the next day or two,' Tim said. 'We're running short of food.'

'We can go a long time without eating if we have to,' I said.

'That may be true if a person is in good shape,' Tim said. 'But we aren't.' He held up my arm and pinched it just below the elbow. The bone stood out in sharp relief. 'Maybe I made a mistake,' he said. 'Maybe we should have stayed at the cabin.'

'And risk having that Sharp come back and kill us? Oh no, Tim. We're better off here.'

He started to say something, but closed his mouth instead.

We set off early in the morning and hadn't taken a hundred steps when we were out of the trees and into a clearing. No, it wasn't a clearing. It was a field! Some human hand had shaped this vast, treeless slope. We struggled through the snow, and Tim stopped.

'Lizzy,' he said, his voice trembling. 'Feel this.'

I reached down under the snow, near his leg. Yes, there was no mistaking it. We had come upon a barbed wire fence.

We got over it and, as we breasted a small hill, he pointed.

'Look!'

Down below us, ramshackle and worn, unpainted and humble, yet as glorious as the finest castle in Camelot, was a farmhouse. And pointing up at us and plunging through the snow were two men.

We hurried to meet them. One was old and the other young. Both were amazed.

'Where do you two think you're going?' asked the older one.

'Indian Lake,' I said. 'We live there.'

'Indian Lake is sixty miles from here,' said the other man. 'What were you doing in the woods?'

I told them we had been canoeing down Cold River and had lost our canoe. The older man interrupted. 'When was that?'

'October the seventeenth,' I said. The young one started to ask another question, but the older one shook his head and said, 'We got to get these young'uns in where it's warm. Come on, little girl, let me carry you. '

I looked at him and at Tim who was grinning and crying, both at the same time, and said: 'No, thank you, sir. If it's all the same to you, we'd rather walk the rest of the way.'

That was long ago. But not within my mind, where the memories remain, as vivid and alive as ever they were. And not in my heart, where I always knew the truth, although I didn't ever speak it out, not even to Indian Pete, who questioned me at length once we were home.

'We searched all over those mountains,' he said. 'We didn't find the road your father took until snow flew. By then we couldn't get down the creek. Little girl, how did you stay alive all those months?'

I never spoke of the cabin, and neither did Tim. I knew, without asking, why he had burned it down. I knew without his ever telling me what was in that shed he wouldn't let me enter. Often, in my nightmares, I have seen him, trembling in the darkness with an old shotgun and one homemade shell, waiting for Sharp to open the shed door, and wondering whether the gun would fire. I never spoke of it to Tim or to anyone else.

Now, of course, it doesn't matter.

When my plane landed in Buffalo there was a car waiting for me. It took me right out to the 'senior village' where Tim had been living for the past three years. I would have preferred something less like an institution, but it was Tim's money. If he chose to spend it on this impersonal lump of concrete and faceless people, instead of moving to Sarasota as I had urged, that was his business. I had no right to interfere. But if only I could have, I was primed to hand him another hot argument on the subject.

Mrs Samantha Gilbert, the manager, was waiting for me. We had never met, so I didn't blame her for asking: 'We got your wire, but would you mind telling me, Mrs Allison, are you a relative?'

'It is *Miss* Allison. And, yes, I am indeed a relative. Tim Hood is my brother.'

'But –'

I brushed past her and went in.

He was so natural and lifelike that it was all I could do to keep from yelling at him: 'Stupid! Why didn't you tell me you were sick?' But there will come a time soon when I can do that, I'm sure. Instead I bent over and kissed his cheek. Then, just before I closed the lid, I whispered: 'Don't you worry about another thing, Timmy. I've come to take you home.'

Z for Zachariah

ROBERT O'BRIEN

Put yourself in Ann Burden's position. She is sixteen. She believes she is the last person left alive on Earth. For over a year, since the atomic world war and its annihilating after-effects, she has not dared leave the valley where she lives, which has somehow escaped radiation poisoning. Her family went in search of help soon after the bombing, but did not return. She is utterly, completely, alone.

But one day a man comes into the valley, wearing a radiation-proof suit. Ann has no way of knowing how trustworthy or sane he is. At first she is hopeful, but then begins the grim contest between them for survival.

Told in diary form, Ann's story is gripping, relentless and terrifying.

'The cool documentation and stark, simple flow of the narrative have a tremendous force behind them.'

Margery Fisher

Newbery Award winner Robert O'Brien is the author of *The Silver Crown*, also available in Lions.

Alan Garner

THE WEIRDSTONE OF BRISINGAMEN
THE MOON OF GOMRATH
ELIDOR
THE OWL SERVICE

When Alan Garner's first book, *The Weirdstone of Brisingamen*, was published he was hailed by reviewers as a great new writer. *The Weirdstone* and its sequel *The Moon of Gomrath* are fantasies of striking imagination and power set around Alderley Edge in Cheshire where Alan Garner lives.

With the publication of *The Owl Service* Alan Garner received both the Guardian Award and the Carnegie Medal. Set in Wales, the story describes the reawakening of an ancient legend of jealousy and destruction which threatens to live again in Alison, Roger and Gwyn.

Alan Garner has been described in the *Times Educational Supplement* as 'one of the most exciting writers for young people today. He is producing work with strong plot structure, perceptive characterisation and vivid language. Furthermore, there is in his writing a basic integrity within which the poetic imagination may have free rein. It is a combination of qualities that creates literature that will be read and read again.'